Cherish Desire Singles:

Sexy Identities Collection 1

Written by

Max D

brought to you by Cherish Desire

DEDICATION

This book is dedicated to all the amazing spirits I have encountered while wandering.

Always pursue a better world. The stars are watching.

CONTENTS

Erotic Themes

This book is intended for mature audiences. Cherish Desire books contain erotica adventures featuring intense sexual situations including alternative lifestyles, perverse pleasures, and supernatural lust.

"Sexy Identities 1: A Captain & A Fairy" themes: Cosplay, MF, Romance, Vaginal Sex

"Sexy Identities 2: Engineer Urges" themes: Female Masturbation, Vaginal Penetration, Femdom, D/s, Bondage & Restraints, Implied Cosplay, Implied Rubber & Latex & Fetish Wear, Implied Vaginal & Oral Sex, Implied Punishment Play

"Sexy Identities 3: Unicorn Kisses" themes: Cosplay, Bodypaint, FF, Implied D/s, Wax Play, Vaginal & Oral Sex

"Sexy Identities 4: Wanting The Bat" themes: Cosplay, MF, MM, Vaginal & Oral & Anal Sex, Vaginal & Anal Penetration, Object Insertion (Hammer Handle, Police Baton), Fingering & Fisting, Bondage & Restraints

"Sexy Identities 5: To Serve The Worthy" themes: MF, Supernatural & Paranormal, Vampire, Romance, Blood Play, Sitophilia & Food Fetish

"Sexy Identities 1: A Captain & A Fairy"

written by Max D

Featuring the Lovers of Sexy Identities

"Sexy Identities 1: A Captain & A Fairy" themes:
Cosplay, MF, Romance, Vaginal Sex

I tucked my arms in and made myself as small as possible, shrinking nearly to the size that I am inside my head, as soon as I heard the heavy thud of combat boots slamming into the floor right behind me. If I had squeezed my eyes shut any tighter then I am sure that I would have wet myself. I was wobbly – maybe even tipsy - from three too many vodka cranberries, and I was all alone on the dancefloor swimming through the throngs of weird dancers while shooting at them with my glitter wand and giggling like a maniac. After pointing him out, after being scolded for being judgmental, after swearing to stay away... somehow, I had ended up in the path of this raging lunatic who sliced through the crowd like his hands were swords and he owned the place.

Powerful hands swept over my shoulders, just ghosting my outline and barely touching me, and I cringed while shaking in my cute Mary Janes. A low growl roared like a thunderstorm rolling in from the sea and passed over my head as his body twisted around me before he catapulted himself into a weaving group of ravers with neon-coloured afro wigs and bright spandex bell bottoms. I was still paralyzed, frozen in place and holding my breath, when my Captain's arm slid around my shoulders. He comforted me with a gentle squeeze and led me away while laughing at my attempt to play statue still in the moment the militant dancer had come within inches of crushing me like a little ladybug.

I was still shaking after two more vodka and cranberries when I saw him drop to his feet and suddenly transform from an irrational killing machine to a normalish looking human. There was still a touch of something mechanical in how he moved, and I couldn't help but stare at his body flexing and shifting like the muscles under his tight fitting shirt were somehow independently alive and testing the restraints of their cage. "You're going to make him come over here," my Captain murmured with a chuckle. I wasn't sure if it was a prediction or an order... and he was right. Running a strong hand through his thinning hair, the mecha-man came right over to us.

He sized my Captain up with a glance and grinned. "You both look great tonight. Captain Hook and Tinkerbell. Classic. Very cool." Then he looked over at me, and I was shrinking into my Captain's chest, hoping I could will myself to fairy size and then escape to hide at the nape of my Captain's neck or duck under his hat. "Sweetie, I know you're having a good time, but please be careful where you're going. I dance in straight lines. It's a very predictable pattern. I really wrenched my back trying to avoid colliding with you earlier, and I might not have enough space to maneuver like that next time." Then he smiled at us both, and the dark flash in his eyes was a bit too bright even with his glasses covering up his unnatural radioactive glow. "Have a great convention. Watch out for monsters."

My Captain remained dead silent. We'd come out to the costume convention on a mutual whim, but it was my idea to go dancing in the evening and so long... much longer than I'd realised... into the night. My Captain is more of a lover and a talker. He isn't a huge fan of the electronic music that I like to dance to: he complains that the heavy bass and percussion loops make him edgy. With his history, how could I blame him? Add that to the mad man's warning, and I think we would have been headed out the door if my Captain wasn't trying to process it all in his typical deliberate manner. He prefers to puzzle things out, to understand them, and to visualize the destination and path while pondering intentions.

Me? I was already thinking 'Tick Tock Tick Tock.' I was shuddering and terrified by the synchronicity of it all. Mind the monsters? What had the mechanical dancer said to me before? "I forgive you, little wand." Or was it "little one?" I fingered the big glittering white star on the end of my wand, suddenly infected with drunken silliness, and I lifted it up while snuggling into my Captain's ribs. Taking aim, I whispered, "Pow pow pow... pow... pow pow," glitter sniping everyone dressed in bright colours.

My Captain seemed to have made up his mind. He tipped his chin and kissed the top of my head. "Why, sweet Tinkerbell... you are quite the precocious brat tonight." I continued sniping while grinning from ear to ear. "Do you think that was my crocodile?" I made a face and turned into my Captain's chest, his big silver jacket buttons pressing into the soft folds of my tight fitting white lace tunic, and squinted at him.

"Pow." I laughed with my wand aimed wildly at the bar patrons nearby. My Captain leaned forward, gracefully kissing me, and I lifted up on my tiptoes to capture his affectionate lips. "Not your crocodile... but if I see him, I'll pow him into oblivion anyway." He brushed his hawkish nose against my check and kissed my earlobe, just catching it with his teeth while I trembled happily as his warm breath caressed me.

Whispering just loud enough for me to hear, my Captain said, "Aye. With a glitter cannon and from the safety of my pirate ship. He won't take me from you, my precious Tinkerbell, or you from me."

I giggled, still giddy. "Ka-boom. Boom boom boom..." and I couldn't help myself as I wiggled and swayed against my Captain's fine coat and soft breeches. The echoing roar of the music filled me with desire and purpose. I was the tiny and forceful embodiment of magic that even monsters respected. I was my Captain's protector. I was damn sexy, and my little asymmetric skirt was wonderfully slinky and caressed my thighs and buttocks when I moved just right.

Shaking his head and fixing his proud hat, my Captain hugged me close and began to lead us toward the door. Away from the steady beat. Away from the monster man. Toward the peace and quiet of his quarters where he would ravage me and I would respond with the heated fever of a lusty cabin boy. I went without question, following my Captain with my wand at the ready, and we stalked the silent streets with a swagger and a hearty laugh all the way to our hotel. I stood at the ready and guarded his back. He spoke loudly of our successful shore excursion. We plotted opening a bottle of rum and toasting our adventure.

In my Captain's arms as soon as the elevator's doors closed, I pursued his kisses with my heart fluttering in my chest. His strong hand cradling my bottom and lifting me up would have made my wings unfurl if I had any. Instead, my ankles crossed and toes curled as my poor panties were soaked while my Captain swept me off my feet and decided to carry me across the threshold and into our room. I even got to take my time groping about in his pockets looking for our card key.

Oh, the things my Captain does to me. I swoon when he whispers to me, sharing his perverse desires, and then lowers me sweetly onto his bed. I caress his mast and unfurl my sails as he lifts me from the doldrums of reality, sails me to our own place where I am the nymph that he can't resist and he is the rogue whose darkness I find irresistible. He plunges his sword deep and demands that I provide a willing sheathe for his needs, as if I would ever turn him away. With my pretty skirt pushed up to my waist and my dainty sex exposed, my Captain gathers me to him and I willing press my body to his. The seas stir within me - wet waves of lust and pleasure soaking hardened wood and prow. He praises my graceful maneuvering, and I joyfully moan in response to his masterful handling.

As fingertips stroke my nipple, my tiny body twists with the suddenness of a sail snapping in the wind. My Captain illuminates me from within and sensations sparkle under my skin. He watches my soft, pale red lips as I kiss the firm, flesh-coloured synthetic skin of his prosthesis. I whisper into the silence of his eyes, and he laughs, and we don't ever talk about all the pain my Captain has been through. I'm his Tinkerbell, after all. I'll watch over him and take care of him even when the nightmares terrorize him with percussive explosions and that dreaded feeling of compressed bass suddenly enveloping his body and hurling him away from the blast of an IED.

I carefully push his beautiful coat from his shoulders and caress his chest through his white cotton shirt. He is my Captain. His heart beats for me, and the fact it shouldn't makes it all the more precious. He holds still while I explore his desire and my need. I want him stripped so I can kiss his scars and make him whole. I want to feel his tongue licking at my petite peach. I want to take his sadness, touch it with my wand, and magic it into dust. I want to ride the hard mast of his cock until he knows nothing but my enveloping wetness. I perch on his shoulders and look over his beautiful body as if I was in a crow's nest looking for familiar shores... and happily finding them.

He laughs, recognising the wanton look that I always get when we're alone, and my Captain slowly helps me undress him. When it's my turn, I wiggle with impatience while wordlessly helping my Captain undo my skirt and tunic. When he sets my clothes at the end of the bed, I can't help looking for my wand. My Captain laughs when he hands it to me, enjoying how I grin like I've been given my first taste of chocolate on my birthday.

With a beckoning wave over his beautiful body, I summon my Captain out loud with a flick of my wand. "As you wish," he winks with a happy smile. The darting motion of his tongue wetting his lips emphasizes that he is a treasure hunter who has spied his ultimate bounty. My Captain slips over top of me and then rolls onto his back so I can straddle his shaft and set sail again. For him, I'm a lusty wench, a pirate's whore, and I ride the swells that rock the bed beneath us with glee. The forbidden nature of our love, the secrecy and the taboo of the liaison between fairy and fiend, is just dirty enough to press into the sheets like a firm lusty wind and drive us forward. My pleasure slips across his hips as we navigate through the swells and troughs together, and I hold fast to his chest as my Captain claims his Tinkerbell and we are joined in a storm of passion.

We laugh and cuddle and bite and struggle, and I wiggle and squirm while pressing hard against my Captain's firm body. He pinches my petite buttock while holding me onto him. The throbbing of his lust flows into my sex with the force of a summer squall. I am soaked in the suddenness of his bountiful release, and, with careful navigation, I hold him fast while my Captain rests beneath me. He yields the helm to me, and I carefully guide us to shore while tenderly caressing his grizzled cheek.

We never saw the monster again, but we never forgot him. "My Tinkerbell," my Captain will say proudly to anyone who will listen, "can charm even a monster's fury." And then he tells the story of how impish little me, with just my tiny glitter wand, single-handedly defeated a monster warrior of such ferocity that hippies whispered of the Jabberwocky and other such things in his wake. His pride always makes my chest swell, and I never correct him. I simply lift my glitter wand up and whisper, "Pow," with a wink.

Well. That's the story anyway though it's not entirely true. Not just my Captain's glorious rendition of my bravery and careful aim as I struck down the dangerous landlubbers with my sparkly wand until I had fired my last shot and then we had to flee to our waiting dinghy and row mightily to where our great pirate ship was hidden in a secluded cove. Not just that.

I met the monster again. The very next day, in fact. He was with a gorgeous slender unicorn who smiled with the dazzling light of a million full moons while sweeping back her long chestnut hair. The

"Sexy Identities 1: A Captain & A Fairy"

monster saw me immediately, and... he waved. I didn't know what to do, and my Captain was away fetching provisions, so I stayed on my perch as I was ordered, but I was panicking and shaking with fear. The monster and unicorn approached, coming directly for me, and I could not escape.

With soft words that murmured of dreamlands full of mystical powers, his unicorn companion flowed over me, and I was mesmerized by her grace and smile. "So you're the Tinkerbell," her words caressed the air with the grace of a painter's brush stroking over fresh canvas. "You really are delightful." Her eyes were so bright that I could see my own reflection in them.

I lifted my glitter wand and aimed it right at her heart. "Pow..." I said, and then I giggled.

Unicorns... they give the sweetest kisses. Her long hair cascaded over me and I was flushed in the sudden heat of her presence as she kissed my forehead. "You're so pretty," she murmured while lingering close and we sipped the same heated air for a moment. Then the beautiful unicorn straightened up while blushing bright red, and I laughed as she stammered out an excuse about being tired and up too late and having never been so intimate with a complete stranger ever before.

The monster swept in beside her with a cautious hand lifted to her elbow. "Let's go, Jess," he gave her a gentle squeeze, and then turned to me. "It was good seeing you again. Tell your Captain that I was happy to share the floor with someone who had served. Have a great weekend." There was something terrible in his easy confidence and brutal awareness. Something that reminded me of the beasts who order others into battle and then tally the wounded and dead while pursuing endless calculations to seek an advantage no matter what the cost.

I never told my Captain about that. About the unicorn or the monster. We don't talk about things that bring back the bad memories. I'm his Tinkerbell and my wand and my loyalty will protect him from all the terrors that matter. Even a monster knows I mean business.

"Sexy Identities 2: Engineer Urges"
written by Max D

Featuring the Lovers of Sexy Identities

"Sexy Identities 2: Engineer Urges" themes: Female Masturbation, Vaginal Penetration, Femdom, D/s, Bondage & Restraints, Implied Cosplay, Implied Rubber & Latex & Fetish Wear, Implied Vaginal & Oral Sex, Implied Punishment Play

When I watched "Chronicles of Riddick," I imagine that I had the same hot flashes every sexually eager woman had. Vin Diesel was cut and gorgeous. It didn't matter if the movies had any substance beyond his muscular body, and, of course, my favorite scene was Riddick slumping onto the Necromongers throne. I could watch that bit over and over again. In fact, I did watch that over and over when the movie came out on bluray, hit pause at just that moment, enjoyed the rush of fevered inspiration that made my toes tingle, and it took many afternoons and evenings to use it up to be honest. I was bummed out about that last bit until along came Prometheus, and I recognized that maybe I had a problem.

I had expected to indulge in my lust of all things macabre and dark, so an Aliens movie was a mandatory thrill! I had watched the trailer with the strange denuded albino male dissolving himself into the cascading waterfall, but that didn't put me off. I had expected something spooky and disturbing, and I made cinema plans with friends as soon as there was a release date. We were there early because I was not going to miss any of the action. Then I suffered through the slow beginning with my idle hands scratching at the arms of my chair. Things didn't seem to even get started until the expedition landed and I really wasn't happy until things finally got interesting in the off-world caverns. The familiar buzz of anticipation made me shiver in my seat when the crew encountered the evolving snake-like aliens. My expectations had been lowered, and it was just going to be an ok movie in my opinion. Still, that was alright.

Then the crew discovered the Engineer pilot. That initial scene with the broad vistas of an alien flight deck was everything that I enjoy about science fiction and horror blended together. The discovery of a living Engineer was a concept that I was intrigued by, and that I hadn't been expecting. My pulse sped up, and I found myself far more swept up in the developing story than I thought I'd be. When the sarcophagus opened, when this immensely strong and statuesque man was birthed into the movie, I thought that I was suffering from a bout of mild delirium brought on by horror-induced euphoria. I felt flushed and vibrant, and my heart was pounding in my chest.

Trembling while holding onto my seat, suddenly realizing how heavily I was breathing, fighting to keep quiet in the cinema, I looked over at my friends. They seemed so calm, almost bored, and I couldn't understand it. My mind was racing. Peter was trying to silently slurp up the last of his soda, and Priya was draped over her armrests and slumped in her seat. I tried to cross my legs to calm my racing pulse, but that rubbed my labia together and out of nowhere I realized that I was turned on. Really turned on. Their heat kindled the growing fire within me, and I let my mind loose to explore the concepts that had set my fantasies aflame: the arousal of fear, the intimidating presence of the alien supreme being, and the idea of being stranded and lost while at the mercy of this deity-like creature. On the screen, the Engineer attacked, violently asserting his dominance and strength, and I almost whimpered while imagining him wrapping his massive hand around my throat. Peter petted my arm, but thankfully didn't look at me close enough to realize I was blushing bright red and holding my breath to keep from hyperventilating. He thought that I'd flinched in my seat because I was frightened, but I was thrumming with desire. It was how that monstrous man moved - how he decisively strode into action - it just confirmed everything I'd developed hyper-speed fantasies about. I struggled to avoid blatantly straining to see what I needed to see so badly.

The thought of his slightly bluish white cock - long and thick and formed with bulging veins that pulsed and writhed along the length of his shaft like snakes under his skin - took up every conscious thought while the Engineer sat in his command console and began hunting for his trajectory. With perspiration prickling my skin and threatening to drip down my cleavage, I had to excuse to the bathroom. I had to escape. I had to get into the light, to splash cold water onto my face, and to have time to myself. I wobbled out to the multiplex hallway on my shaky legs and then rushed to the ladies restroom.

I had no choice. I had to hurry because I was pretty sure there was a growing wet spot in the seat of my trousers. In the stall, I thought for a few seconds about trying to calm myself down before jettisoning logic and giving in to the demands of my body. With one arm braced against the door, my forehead resting in the crook of my elbow, I unbuttoned my jeans and dipped my hand down to feel the wetness that was seeping into my panties. I meant to draw it out. It wasn't as if I was worried about being caught. I'm not all that loud - well, I'm not shy - and there was nobody around. But as soon as I began to push my fingers back and forth over the slick, swollen nub of my clit, I knew I had no hope of slowing down. I blocked conscious thoughts out, ignored the thrill of masturbating in public, and just let the images that had inspired my imagination flit through my mind. The Engineer's perfection, and the heady combination of fear and desire in his presence made me buck against my hand. My eyes moved as I imagined his graceful form, the power of his rippling muscles, and the massive endowment that I would need to satisfy. Fingers drumming and rubbing with urgent need surging through them, I orgasmed with a shuddering sigh, and my legs threatened to give out completely and dump me on the bathroom floor.

Just like that: the image was fixed in my mind. It became a fetish and an obsession: something that I needed.

At the time, I didn't know Priya well. Peter, I think, understood that I am all about Aliens in my own perverse way though, and he thought I might have gotten ill when I didn't return until the end of the movie. Rather than asking any questions about what happened, he offered to take me back out again sometime. We all have monthly movie passes, so we can watch as many showings as we want. Peter drives so it's not too difficult for him to pick me up and take me to the cinema. It's more about having company and somewhere to hang out.

In this case, I had to pass. I did say that I'd like to watch the movie at home though. Peter is one of those really kind and funny sorts of guys, and he remembers everything, so I wasn't all that surprised that he made sure I had the bluray release as soon as it came out. Until that moment, I had done everything that I could to avoid the posters and trailers and commercials about Prometheus because I was fighting my own lusty urges. Part of me wanted to savour the pay-off that would be watching the rest of the film, and part of me was just a bit disturbed by the whole thing. I explained away everything with sly comments about the alluring adrenalin spike of fear and surprise at the well-executed Engineer costume. My hot flush in the cinema and the weird fixation that I'd developed since were just lingering side effects of a movie that I mostly didn't watch because I left so soon. I had distracted myself with loads of other things, and I've got plenty at home and at work to keep me busy. Plus my mum to deal with... she's a real pain in my kitty ears, let me tell you! But I wasn't about to write my strange flight of fantasy off entirely, and I waited until late that evening, when my family were fast asleep, and then slipped Prometheus in.

The bluray disc slid so comfortably into my player, like a favourite dildo slipping into a willing pussy. My heart was already beating faster from excitement, and my fingers trembled as I held the remote. Although I hadn't realised it until that point, it was so obvious that under the surface my fantasies were queued for action. I pressed play. I skipped past the beginning of the movie, no longer caring about the Aliens plot. I wanted to see the Engineer, to watch him move, and to study every curve of his freakishly large and deliciously detailed body.

I was not disappointed. In just the kitty ears and my loose Disney pajamas that I like to wear when I'm alone, I watched that muscle-bound giant rise from his slumber. I watched him lash out, and his fury made my breathing come shallow and fast. I watched the rhythm of his heart pulse through his body, and his life-force wet my inner thighs. I watched the corded meat of his forearm flex under his impossibly smooth and tight alabaster skin, and his enormous proportions made it necessary to spread my feet wide apart so I could straddle him. I was lost in my own dreams, the constellations whirling around us as I slipped into his lap and rode his massive cock, all while he silently raged against the universe.

This was the moment when I had fled the movie theatre. Everything after this scene was new to me. I had to watch as the pathetic humans did their best to counter my muscular Engineer. I had to sit through their endless noise and bickering and camaraderie, and I saw how they infuriated him. I knew it would take a strong woman to bring him down: only a woman's passion and determination would be enough. I watched the battle with the proto-alien, and I wasn't even drawn into my usual Geiger-landscaped daydreams. It was just me and my Engineer. It was one of the most satisfying nights of my life.

Obviously and most disappointingly, finding a seven foot tall man was not going to be an option. Finding one with the incredibly hot physique of an Engineer was even less likely. My eye was on the bio-mechanical suit of the Engineer though... that seemed more achievable. I've seen all kinds of restraints and bondage and latex bodysuits, but I had started imagining one that incorporated the protruding ridges and bony carapace of his suit. I imagined the luscious delight of immobilizing the powerful male occupant by locking all the suit joints in place... I imagined his head shaking, trying to resist, as my kitty claws slowly descended to his fitted cod piece and tugged away the only protective layer between me and his heavy cock...

and suddenly my little Alien kink had taken on a whole new dimension.

It would be me - in my thigh high black latex boots, hot pants, and tube top wrap - that would feel the texture of his bodysuit stroking over my smooth abdomen. I'd command him, demand his pleasure, and use my sharp nails to make the urgency of my satisfaction clear. My superbly-developed Engineer would need to comply or risk losing what he once believed was his most important appendage. When I slid over his chest, unbuttoning the side of my shorts, and lowered my pussy onto his tongue, then he'd understand that human women were superior to his technology and brute force. He'd understand or he'd gasp for air trying to breathe while I slowly fucked his face and clawed at his cock. Perhaps both.

Would it be his fault for not being seven or eight foot tall with an enormous specimen between his legs? Maybe. Mostly it would just be for my pleasure, my sheer delight at having captured an obedient spaceman to serve my delicious desires and fantasies. I'd put on "Big Bad Wolf" and listen to Daniel sing while wetting my captive's lips with my sex. I'd roll my hips and grind my tender labia over his chin and mouth. I'd lean forward, nipping and biting at his exposed pelvis and cock, just threatening with my teeth while thrusting onto his extended tongue. I'd press my lean body against his bulging xenotechnology suit while laughing as his fingers scratched at the bed in the fight for control, though whether it would be over the whole situation or just over himself, he'd never know. My completely immobilized giant's gorgeous muscles would strain to escape as my sharp teeth controlled the motion of his massive body.

But it was more than that. I watched the Engineer's scenes over and over, binging on endorphins as I pinched and stroked my tender labia, rubbed at my clit, and writhed against the soft brushed cotton of my bedclothes. It contrasted so nicely with the nip of my nails, and the deliberately too-hard nudges of my fingers. I enjoy the intensity and spike of adrenaline when I'm playing rough. I enjoy teeth on my skin. I get wet when I have a new piercing done. My fantasy Engineer filled me with fresh lust while I conjured up the sensations of being bruised on the inside by his enormous cock and having imprints of his fingers when I allowed him to hold me. I soaked my pajamas and my fingers and my duvet cover.

I needed it. I needed him, and I could accept a facsimile if I had to. Just to soften the sharp edge of my hunger. I wanted the real thing though, of course: I wanted him to understand my perfection and power exactly the way I am. I'd be standing naked above him, leering at his massive prone form and feeling the moisture gathering in the soft folds of my pussy lips. I would ride him and break him and make my Engineer beg while his alabaster skin wept tears of blood from a thousand scratches. I would hammer my pussy onto his pelvis so hard that we were both bruised by my hunger. I would force him to cum, and then ride his face until my juices and his semen covered his bluish lips and chin. I might kiss him like that... if he earned my approval. He'd be bewildered and thrilled, his body providing him with all the instruction he needed... and he'd be entirely mine.

I had to stop after two hours of masturbation made my clit so sore that the tender nub ached without even being touched. My labia were puffy and swollen, scratched and bruised. My fingers were wrinkled with the moisture of my cooling desire, and my nipples were so hard that they seemed like they'd be visible from orbit, peeking and pointing up at my Engineer, wherever he was out there. My urges ravaged my exhausted mind, and I collapsed into my bed while succumbing to unnatural fantasies.

So here's the deal and I'm going to make it very clear. You: tall, fit, built, and powerful. Wearing an Engineer exosuit with all the appropriate Geiger details plus a removable codpiece. You'll find me at AntiChrist or Torture Garden, I'm a regular there... I'd tell you how to identify me, but I'll find you. Who knows, dressed like that you might find another kitten more perverse than you can handle. Respect the kitty and take orders well. In exchange, you will be fucked so hard and so often in that bodysuit that it'll become your second skin. I guarantee it. I'll train your tongue so you can please any woman in the future. I'll claw, nip, whip, and abuse your cock and scrotum until you can get an erection from s single whispered command and know how to please every dominant woman with your readiness. You'll have a pretty kitty on your arm in public to prove you are worthy of other women... if they can even offer something delightfully perverse enough to entice you out of my claws for an evening.

"Sexy Identities 2: Engineer Urges"

As my pleasingly perverted American wolf says, "Just do it." What do you have to lose, Engineer?

His Wulf Daughter is a multiplicity wrapped within the cloaks of her fandoms, fetishes, and fantasies. Read more about her within Miez's stories.

"Sexy Identities 3: Unicorn Kisses"

written by Max D

Featuring the Lovers of Sexy Identities

"Sexy Identities 3: Unicorn Kisses" themes: Cosplay, Bodypaint, FF, Implied D/s, Wax Play, Vaginal & Oral Sex

I choose my colours carefully while biting the tip of my tongue. Blue... so many lovely shades of blue. Black... dark as night and reminder of stealthy hugs. Red... crimson like stolen kisses and bright like flushed cheeks. Greens and aquas... and white as crisp as fresh linens. He's rolling his eyes as I wander back and forth between my make-up and paint palette. I'm fussing and surging with creative urges, and he's steady and calm with eyes that never blink and see everything. I'm not sure he understands how important this part is to me.

I feel exposed. He's always so gentle with me, and I'm always so busy. Nothing will ever happen

"Sexy Identities 3: Unicorn Kisses"

between us. We both know it, feel it, and yet... there he is, right there sitting at the end of my bed while I let my insanity unfold and spread it out around me. Just a friend of a dear friend, and even she had her questions. He doesn't though. His only questions are when I can go to the farmers market, and am I having an okay time, and am I comfortable. Sometimes we talk about art. Sometimes we talk about my masters studies. Sometimes we talk about his work. Then he vanishes.

And randomly I send him a message, a unicorn's transmission of rainbows into the darkness between the stars, and I never know when he'll reply.

I don't think he really understands. Long and willowy, lean and quiet, I've always preferred to hide behind my camera because I've always been noticed. Passionate heat burns through me, and I try to hide it away. I pine for a lovely lady's special kiss. I long for a certain man's fingers caressing my neck. My art gathers within me and explodes outward like coloured fireworks. I smile so hard that my cheeks hurt. I don't think he can ever understand that. He's so dark and determined and powerful and broken.

And when I finally settle into my chaise lounge, black eyeliner pencil in hand, I sweep up my long brown hair and push it back so I can slowly outline my thoughts on my thigh. He's smiling. I never see that. It worries me, and I bite my lower lip while trying to manage a straight line despite my trembling hands. I'm hiding from the pleasure that he's expressing and which I don't understand. He sees me tuck my chin, focus inward, and gets up.

I freeze. "I'm going to head home, Jess," he says so softly that it's barely a sigh. "Unless you want me to stay." It's not a guilt trip, but I feel obliged to say something to reassure him.

When I look up, I realize that he's smiling at something that I can't even see: something bigger than me. Something important to him. His world is so far away from my rainbows and moons and sparkling stars. "Ummmm, okay." I don't need to tell him to stay. He's happy. He's never happy, but, for some reason that I cannot fathom, he looks content and pleased.

With a gentle squeeze of my shoulder, he lets himself out. Out of my room. Out of the house that I share with my nana. Out into the world where he will vanish into some distant orbit, where unicorn posters gather and he loads them into a rocket ship and launches them toward me....to make me smile. To make me laugh. To remind me that he sees me.

I go back to drawing and painting on my pale skin. The brushes tickle and the paints and colours transform me bit by bit from artist into art. The change begins like a soft kiss on the lips; my hair falling forward as I turn and twist. The change flows from the thin wooden wand that leaves colourful trails on my skin as I begin to become a butterfly. It takes patience and time. It takes extra long brushes and mirrors and no small amount of contortionism. It takes the quiet of my room and the familiarity of all my things around me and the peaceful ebb and flow

"Sexy Identities 3: Unicorn Kisses"

of time that carries me forward from moment to moment.

A friend of a friend. I'm biting my lip again, my face twisted in concentration. I remember her soft sighs and slow kisses - and how much I longed for them before I even knew what they'd feel like on my lips and skin. I remember sitting and waiting for her next great plan. I remember how brave and amazing she always was. So much bigger than life. Her petite body fitting into the curve of mine, and I would wish her into a cuddly teddy bear and sleep so well just thinking of her in my arms. She was also devious and daring... but her charms came with a cost. Working so hard and adored by everyone, she had to be careful. Men can be so demanding. Women are just as possessive and sometime much more venomous than vipers. I hid behind my camera, so happy when she'd go for a shoot with me, and I adored her as much as anyone else could.

Only a pixie could charm a unicorn, and I nickered and pawed the ground in restless hope of her affection. Her eyes lit up as she lassoed my pale neck, collaring me before leaning in close, and I was hers when she whispered, "Hot wax first." Her delicious deviousness made my long legs shiver, and I obediently followed her as if I was bewitched. Her tiny hands guided me to my bed, and her soft kisses seduced me. Her heat made me blush as she transformed me into her beautiful steed.

Slowly stripped bare, exposed and on fire, she teased my timid lust as I tried to hold back. She placed my hands on her petite bottom while she gyrated and danced against me, and every time I gasped for more she kissed my tender lips. The scratching of matches being struck made me shiver, and the candles bright flames flickered. I tried to escape her in a desperate act of resistance, but her petite fingers took hold of my collar. Hazel eyes twinkling, she stared straight through my closed eyelids and into my frightened heart. "My unicorn beauty." I was lost in love and only her hand could steady me. Only her control kept me from becoming insubstantial and slipping away with each gasp of breath. Only my pixie's pink lips led to the rainbow that I needed to sustain me.

Love is such a treacherous thing when you have the heart of a unicorn and the body of a woman. I love completely and fully without reservation. I love with every breath and every happiness and every sorrow. I am drawn to beauty and pleasure. I am a smile waiting to be bestowed with a kiss.

Even now I am plunged into that moment. The hot wax stings and pools on my breasts, and she is straddling my hips while I sing sweet accolades for her praise. My pixie torments me with extremes, and then makes it all better with a kiss and eager fingers. I don't even know what it means to have her collar on my neck - is it just to scare off would be suitors? - but I have so many hopes for much more than that. Curled up on my chest, the wax sticking to her bare skin, she soothes me with lyrical poetry delivered to my cheeks and lips.

I have to fight the urge to get up, to paint, to sing,

to dance around... She fills me with the desire to move; to wrap the world around me like a cloak before going off to cavort with the moon. Her words become nibbles, her nibbles become licks, and my pixie consumes me with her mouth pressed to my flesh. I am shaking and trying so hard not to kick, but the fluttering within my belly makes it impossible to hold still. My pixie is no virgin; her skillful handling of my womanhood leaves me defenseless and weak from recurring pleasures. The sweet honey of my release has wet her chin and cheeks when she slips over my body and kisses my forehead.

All I can think of is whether it's my turn yet. I know. I am overpowered by her lust and desire, and purity is in the eye of the beholder. Laughing with me as she salaciously wiggles and grinds against my belly, her hands guide mine to her tongue. She wets my fingertips and presses them to her petite breasts. She paints herself with the moist caresses of my passion.

And I take over. She welcomes my touch like a blank canvas waiting to become beautiful. She encourages my fervent fondling with soft sighs and low moans. She becomes still as a statue and then erupts into motion as I slowly evoke the passions of sweltering summers and wetness of ocean depths. I call upon my palette of rich colours, and daub her with fingerpaint like a caveman pleased with the rewards of his hunt. Her scent fills my lungs, and I am breathing in the heavens. Her racing heartbeat drums against my lips, and I am suckling at life itself.

Her petite body flexes and twists, and I capture her within my long hair while pushing her into my bed.

I sense her moment of hesitation. We are pixie and unicorn. We have both been pursued aggressively by those who wish to take their pleasure from us. We have been beneath them. We have lived in fear of their taciturn hearts and rage. Her doubt frightens me and I back away, feeling guilty and hurt. How could I be so terrible? How could I take from the smile that I cherish and need so much? I'm nearly in tears, and I feel stupid and horrible for being so inconsiderate.

My pixie looks up at me, searching out my heart even as I try to hide myself away, and her delicate fingers caress my bare hip. "Oh, sweetie," she murmurs, "you were twisting my knee." I know it's a lie, but I want to believe it. I want to plead with her, to promise that next time I'll be more careful, but she pushes up into me and hugs me so tight that I can't say a word. My quiet tears wet her short blonde hair, and her moist lips heal my wounded heart.

I'm almost done now. The paints flow over my pale skin like a river flowing through a forest and out to the sea. He could have stayed, but then I would have been thinking about him watching me instead of remembering my pixie's comforting embrace. Maybe he understood that. Maybe, in his own strange way, he's afraid of crowding my passions with his presence. I don't know really.

A unicorn never understands what a monster feels.

"Sexy Identities 4: Wanting The Bat"

written by Max D

Featuring the Lovers of Sexy Identities

"Sexy Identities 4: Wanting The Bat" themes: Cosplay, MF, MM, Vaginal & Oral & Anal Sex, Vaginal & Anal Penetration, Object Insertion (Hammer Handle, Police Baton), Fingering & Fisting, Bondage & Restraints

With one arm slung across his new friend's broad shoulders, the purple-suited villain leaned in close and whispered, "I want to be the one to put a big smile on your face." The armored vigilante was covered from head to toe in dull black, his cape hanging straight to the floor, and he continued walking without any outward expression. "I've got exactly what you need..." the fiend nudged the impressive collection of pouches on the dark knight's utili-belt and laughed, "and you've got the tools."

"Oh, sheesh, not again, Mr. J," muttered a shapely

woman in a tight fitting black and red lycra jester costume. "Come on now. Leave the Batman to his business so we can get some Subway. I'm craving some dry meat and lettuce on a long piece of bread to put into my mouth." She was dead serious about satisfying her hunger, but as soon as she tried to take hold of her companion's white-gloved hand, he mocked her with a sneer and cuddled up close against the armored torso of the object of his affection.

"She doesn't understand. We've been places. We've seen things. We've both been caged, ummm... bats... and we need to spread our wings. All those years you spent on your own, all the time I spent in the asylum, left to our own devices... heh... with just the murmurings of lesser creatures to keep us company." He played hard because this was one Batman that he wanted to lose some sleep with. "How about we ditch the dames and go get rowdy? Just you and me. Don't worry. It's not your mask that I want to take off."

Harley Quinn pulled out her massive mallet and didn't bother with a threatening warning. The constant babble of come-ons was just too much, even for her. With one fell swoop delivered to the center of his shoulders, she crumpled her Joker's crisp purple suit and drove him to his knees. White gloved hands slid down the armored legs of his Batman, but the masked vigilante walked away, seemingly uninterested and disconnected from the muttered curses and veiled threats that Harley used to emphasize her immediate need for sustenance that far outweighed the importance of her Joker's urge for sexual satisfaction.

Furious at being denied and rejected, his purple coat tails flapped through the air as the Joker jumped to his feet, spun around to face her fury, and put up his dukes. "Oh, so you want a fight, Mr. J? I got right what you need then!" Harley roared as she lifted her hammer and her heavy breasts strained the tight fitting torso of her bodysuit. He dodged the first blow as a crowd of onlookers gathered with cameras flashing. Encircled, the Joker and Harley Quinn battled and hurled invective from the sixties at one another with glee. A certain amount of caution was obvious in their public confrontation: nothing was said that was blatant enough to be offensive to younger ears and every blow was staged with a certain comic grace despite Harley clearly relishing how she dropped the Joker to his knees repeatedly with hammer blows to his torso and shoulders.

Exhausted and seizing the spotlight, the Joker pleaded with his darling. "Baby, baby, please," he begged from the convention floor, "you know that I just can't stay away from the Batman." She used her mallet like a cane, putting the massive hammer head on the floor while resting her palm on the rounded end of the wooden handle, and crossed her legs while waiting for a proper apology. "We'll get you your Subway. We'll get you whatever you need. It's just... he's my one true weakness."

"Don't you dare say 'Kryptonite,' Mr. J. I know all about your unhealthy affection for men in spandex tights. Why do you think I parade around like this?" She gestured with one hand to emphasize her skintight costume and ample proportions. "Don't you think I'd rather try on a pretty blue dress with a white apron while enjoying the heft of a vorpal blade in my hand?"

"But," now the Joker really seemed to be genuinely affronted, "if you came as mad Alice then... then what would I be? I can't handle being called Angus. It's just too much to ask of me."

A few of the onlookers in the crowd may have appreciated both the references to American McGee's Alice and the role reversal implied by Harley, but it was clear that the rest were mostly interested in seeing Harley Quinn carry on stomping the Joker into further submission. A man in a tail coat with blue satin highlights and tactical trousers with holsters that sported LED edged matt black gear and weaponry pushed through the edge of the crowd, laughed when he saw the Joker on his knees, and swept into the scene to pose with Harley for a few photos. Gesturing with his partially gloved hands, he encouraged other fans to come in and gently positioned Harley to pose triumphantly over her defeated Joker while other convention attendees took their selfies as well. Taking advantage of the pause as another shy couple cautiously approached and shielded him from view, he passed Harley his number. "I would thoroughly enjoy seeing more of you," he murmured coolly and suggested hanging out at one of the after parties. After that photo, with a very proud Kung Fu Panda and Mistress Tigress pair adoringly squeezing in close, the soldier patted 'Mr. J' on the head before marching off with a rolling swagger that made his combat boots thud dully on the smooth floor.

Laughing for the benefit of the onlookers, Harley Quinn pulled the Joker to his feet as the crowd dissipated. "I can't believe you made such a scene," she growled to his ear and made her real feelings clear. The hard edged bite of her jaw made it obvious that she was not pleased and now very, very hungry.

"I'm so sorry, sweetie. It was just going to be a fling. A little afternoon snack. A bit of bat between the cheeks? You know what I mean. You said we could hook up over this weekend after all. You know. With others." With his shoulders sagging under his crumpled purple jacket, the Joker sniffed miserably. "I just wanted a little fun."

"Well, Mr. J," she sighed, "then I guess you should try picking up a 'Batman' that isn't a woman wearing armor to cover up her breasts and thighs." She smacked him affectionately when his eyes opened wide and his jaw dropped. "Just kidding. I think... I think it was a man, anyway..."

With one hand on her mallet and her arm hooked into his, Harley Quinn marched her Joker right up to the Subway queue and then posed while pulling ridiculous faces for all the cameras that were slowly working their way through the Seattle Convention Center while the afternoon passed at PAX. Her hunger needed to be satisfied, but she made sure to discretely poke the softening bulge in her Joker's trousers a few times to remind him to keep his Bat-lust under control.

Hours later, while circling the massive video game booths, she snuck up on the mysterious well-dressed cyberwarrior who'd invaded their battle scene earlier. "Found you," she grinned and shimmied in her Lycra bodysuit while spinning him around. "Now you can tell me what you're dressed as so I won't be thinking about you all weekend." Harley gently pushed on his chest armor as he sized her up. "Unless, of course, you want me thinking about you..."

With a shake of his head and a laugh, he winked at her coy red-lipped smile. He came close enough for his thigh holster to press against her leg. "I'm from the future," his secretive tone was alarmingly well practiced as he gazed into her eyes. "I haven't happened yet." It was either a marvelous cosplay or just a costume that he assembled to fit in at the convention along with a very quick bit of inspired improvisation.

Harley decided that she didn't care. With a dainty kiss and plenty of breast to chest contact, she whispered back, "Is all the future so bold and daring?" His partially gloved hand caressed her hip and held her close. Her next kiss was meant to wow him, and she laughed as he rolled his eyes while pretending to not grind his holster into her inner thigh. Red and white smudges marked his cheek like battle paint, and the heat of contact inspired her own improvisation. "Got a bit of me on you already."

"Not a bad thing," he winked. "But... ummm... your companion..."

Backing out of the soldier's embrace, Harley

"Sexy Identities 4: Wanting The Bat"

Quinn jiggled invitingly. "Oh, Mr. J? He's got a thing for the Batman. A big thing. A thick, swollen, and ridiculously eager thing. That's the only thing that he'll be thinking with this weekend." She offered her hand. "My room or yours? Where exactly does the future begin?"

While Harley was sliding alongside her gentleman warrior as they left the convention center for a more private setting, the Joker hit the jackpot. "Holy dropped bars of soap," he muttered restlessly and adjusted his purple suit trousers. Gathered together for a new video game release were no less than half a dozen Batmen: all buff and spectacularly chiseled in full body armor and capes. Only the rough curves of their mouths were exposed, and Mr. J. was sure that he was being tempted by the devil himself with so many sets of delicious lips placed only a few feet away.

"There he is!" The shout came from behind him, and the Joker instinctively whipped around. Charging through the crowd with some wicked Bat-device in his extended arm and aimed at the helplessly lust addled villain, the Batman from earlier was crying the alarm. "Get him and don't let him escape again!" The other Batmen models stood around, shuffling their feet, and then they realized the crazed cosplay Batman actually expected them to help. The Joker laughed, roaring with pleasure, and then darted off in a chase which he fervently hoped ended up in capture, restraints, and naked pleasures.

"Don't worry! I've got him this time!" The

pursuing Batman darted pasted his brethren, and then charged off in a reckless dash after the purple suited madman weaving through the crowd.

Cheering and laughing followed the cavorting duo as they raced through the convention center. In sudden moments of quiet, they would slow to sneaking about with fingers raised so others wouldn't give them away. Delighted children in costumes ranging from Avengers to Spyro would suddenly shout "There he is!" and the chase would be on again with the Joker leading the way. The staff tolerated a certain amount of tomfoolery, but the purple suited villain guided his Batman through open areas and away from crowded conference rooms to make sure that his delightful chase wasn't interrupted by a blue shirt tossing them out for the rest of the day. After all, putting on a show and appealing to the audience wasn't the point this time. Mr. J. was definitely hoping for more personal satisfaction. After looping three floors of the convention center, he finally made a break for the exit, ditching Batman by the escalators with a run for the elevators instead, and hoped against hope that his pursuer was committed to capturing his prey.

He had his answer while pacing on the sidewalk near the pedestrian crossing. "Joker, you won't get away this time," a booming voice intoned and suddenly the milling crowd of attendees and residents parted as Batman calmly walked up to him. "Put out your hands where I can see them." The deep resonance of the vigilante's voice electrified the crowd and provoked a much more intimate response barely concealed by the villain's trousers.

"Sexy Identities 4: Wanting The Bat"

Whether the Joker was surprised or pleased when black cuffs were fastened around his wrists as soon as his hands were extended in front of his chest, he covered his feelings up well. Most of his attention was on the chiseled cut of Batman's jaw and the blatantly masculine strength beneath the dark black costume. He willingly marched as directed back into the convention center, and then was led out the back entrance and up the hill. More cheering from onlookers as the dark knight had clearly nabbed his man, and the Joker was hoping his pulsating hard-on was at least partially hidden. He couldn't help it after all. He was totally under the Batman's control, and he had no idea where he was being taken.

Despite fantasies of being led to a hidden door leading to a dark cave with all the important comforts of a torture chamber, the Joker wasn't disappointed when he was led into a non-descript hotel lobby. After a long walk in silence, the Batman sighed, tested the cuffs on the Joker's wrists, and pursed his lips in a wry smile. "You gave me one hell of a chase," the masked man laughed softly. "You must have really meant it when you said that you wanted to put a smile on my face."

Blushing under his face paint, the Joker realized that he had been far too direct earlier and almost driven his Batman away. "I definitely mean it." Even at conventions where sexuality was both varied and almost in the open, with innuendo and optimistic banter hinting at the passions bubbling just beneath the surface, immediately sidling up to someone and just presuming that they were bisexual could come across as mocking them. "I couldn't help myself. I've always wanted to be caught." If he could just get a kiss then that would be enough.

"So you play bad boy when you're sweet and innocent on the inside? Yeah, yeah, yeah. Likely story." The powerful man's strong fingers squeezed the Joker's hand - black gloves wrapped around white - and he smirked with his thin lips while his prey gasped. "This is going to get rough, you know."

Aware that his snug boxers were becoming damp with precum, the Joker only murmured, "I wouldn't want it any other way." He only hoped that he could hold out long enough to be sore and aching for the rest of the weekend.

In a more comfortable hotel suite, Harley Quinn was blushing on her freshly made bed as her soldier systematically took off his uniform. From pockets that she hadn't even noticed, he removed a variety of essential objects. From other pouches, he disconnected wiring and harness rigging hooks that powered and held his gear in place. When his tailcoat and chest plate armor came off, his broad chest was enveloped in a matt black stretch shirt that emphasized the shape of his pecs and his strong arms. She hadn't been expecting the solid heft of his build, and her tongue darted over her bright red lips while she admired his physique. When his boots came off, he stood an inch shorter and was a bit closer to her height when she was out of her painted Docs. She held out a hand, gesturing with her fingers for him to come to her, and he only hesitated to remove his belt so the connected holsters wouldn't get in their way. As soon as her long fingers pressed against his ribs, her warrior's heat made her toes tingle.

"I want to wash you first," he whispered while kissing her moist lips. "I seem to have enough make-up on me already."

She giggled. "After you fuck me full of the future, soldier boy." He was both more compact and powerful than Harley had pictured in her head. His jacket and armament had disguised the breadth of his shoulders and mass of his quads. She turned her head from side to side so she could nuzzle his powerful biceps while rubbing off white face paint on his chin.

Her hands slipped over him, and she tugged on his black shirt to lift it up from his waist, and he obliged her. After all, they'd already peeled off her lycra costume to expose the pale curves underneath. "Ah, see..." his fingers stroked over her bare skin and lightly pinched her exposed breasts. "In the future, we enjoy... different things." He was solid, and her sharpened fingernails tested whether he would writhe or complain when she wanted to get rough.

"Oh?" she giggled as he winked in response to her claws raking over his pecs and then sinking into his back. She smeared more red lipstick on his cheek and jaw with pleased wet kisses. "I hope those different things still involve 'Insert Tab A into Slot B.'" He could interpret the specifics of that however he wanted, but Harley wanted to make it very clear that she didn't invite him to her hotel room to order in pizza and play videogames.

His caress drifted lower, tracing the smooth curve of her breasts and skirting over the rounding of her belly, and then he began petting her soft bush. "Well, when dildos became sentient and dangerous, the people of the future became skilled with our fingers... and hands." He delicately stroked over her swollen clitoris while carefully keeping the thin fold of her skin between his fingertips and her pearl. "But you're such a tough woman... I'm sure you can handle more."

She studied his deliberately measured application of strength to her exposed body, in awe of his reserved emotion. Her warrior was clearly in control of everything that he did as he scouted her terrain. Compared to the feverish rush that she was used to, it was almost like participating in a spiritual ritual as he deftly tested her response to pressure, caresses, and pinching. Harley leaned back into a pile of pillows to watch as he marvelously teased her treasure box with his rhythmic touch while looking into her eyes. He was studying her, and she grinned maniacally while pushing her breasts out to distract him. Sliding forward, moving above her, his fingertips parted her tender lips, and his kiss swooped down onto her so his tongue and touch explored her openness in the same moment. She arched her back and thrust against him with glee. He moved with calculated force, ambushing her with suppressing kisses while spreading her moisture onto her labia. She held on tight and pulled him toward her. He shifted tactics when her claws urged him to lose control, and gently scraped his teeth over her chin and neck while

"Sexy Identities 4: Wanting The Bat"

fingering her opening. Her thighs parted as she attempted to capture him. The rough cloth of his tactical trousers pushed against her inner thighs as her soldier willingly fit himself between her legs and used his body to push her knees to the sides. For a moment, she was full of delicious ideas on how to shatter his quiet calm, and then his powerful hands scooped her up and lifted Harley off the pillows. Suspended in mid-air, suddenly twisting in her warrior's powerful embrace, she gasped as he dropped her onto her back and pushed her into the comforter with an audible whoosh. "More..." she hissed when he hesitated while judging her reaction. "Come on! After living with Mr. J. I'm used to a little bit of pain." Her smirk covered up their mutual uneasiness while she unconsciously stared at his broad chest and powerful arms in anticipation.

Pressing two fingers into her quivering pussy, her warrior enjoyed how Harley shook and kicked while he stroked into her sex and pursued her g-spot. His palm cupped her soft bush, rocked against her swollen clitoris, and massaged her labia as he probed deeper into her trembling heat. Her breasts wobbled on her chest, and she swallowed hard as his strong thrusts lightly smacked her pelvis. He acknowledged the heat in her wanton gaze and ignored the way that she was deliberately kicking him to match the tapping of his fingers against her tender pussy walls. Forearm flexing, her soldier took her further as his fingertips stroked over the soft curves and subtle ridges that were hidden within the dark heat of her sex. When he withdrew his wet fingers and lifted them to her lips, Harley sighed and whispered, "I got you covered..." She licked her juices from his fingers, and understood his intentions when he added another finger and waited for her to wet all three.

Their thoughtful exploration and scouting was the exact opposite of the Joker's lusty experience. "I asked if you were going to turn a new leaf," Batman growled and his voice echoed in the stillness of the hotel room, "but apparently you need another lesson." Mr. J. whimpered with agonized satisfaction as Batman pressed the smooth end of a black baton against his anus again. "I got all night... and plenty of patience. I want to see you become a model citizen." He rotated the rigid shaft and grinned as his prey's entire body twisted and shook in response. "What do you say? Maybe give kindness a try..." He pulled the shaft back and then pressed it in again. The baton stuck for a moment, caught on the tender clenching pucker that offered a weak defense before yielding, and then plunged into the Joker's bottom. The villain's entire whole body stiffened and twitched as the black shaft teased his lust.

With his purple suit trousers and bright red satin boxers pushed down to his knees, the Joker managed to gasp, "I think my worst bits are just a tad deeper..." He howled as the Batman forcefully drove the lubricated police-stick another two inches into his rear passage with a firm shove.

Dragging the baton back and then slamming it home again, Batman continued using the Joker's ass as a means to provoke the villain's desires. The masked man could see the way his prisoner's cock leapt and throbbed with every thrust. There was no denying the physical arousal that frosted the tip of the Joker's pulsing erection with slick precum. "Just not good enough. Well, sometimes you just have to do things yourself to make sure they are done right." Leaving the night stick half buried in the Joker's ass, Batman adjusted his costume and folded back a panel along the front of the armoured tights. A hidden zipper was exposed, and Mr. J. looked back just in time to see a heavy Bat-cock released from the padded biker shorts underneath. "Now I've got your attention," Batman muttered while pulling a gold foil condom from his utili-belt pouch. "Don't ever say I held back when there was a chance to convince you to change your ways."

"Reform," the Joker sighed as the baton was tugged from his bottom and he prepared for a thoroughly bat-fulfilling dream come true, "requires deep sacrifices." The sudden surge of the vigilante's swollen cock thrusting into his ass knocked the villain forward and the steel handcuffs bit into his wrists. "Now that's a spicy meatball," he gasped as the first deliberate thrust was followed by a thorough pounding that immediately reddened his buttocks and made his knees weak.

The cybersoldier was also pleasantly surprised: it appeared Harley could take quite the hammering, in addition to giving one out. True, she wasn't quite as practiced as some as his regular ladies, but she accepted his fourth finger with no more than a challenging quirk of one eyebrow and a vicious smack to his cheek. She managed an impressive game face, lewdly thrusting and cheering him on, until he crooked his knuckles just so, levering his fingertips up into her sensitive front wall, and making her back arch. He was rewarded with a subtle but immediate moist flood of her juices coating his fingers and palm, and the flow of her excitement trickled down the valley formed by her swollen labia and moistened her clenching pucker below.

Harley took the tip of his thumb easily, but her warrior slowed down in response to instincts honed by practice, kneading her labia more gently as she began to slip from character and sigh keenly, as he watched the way that she turned her head and pressed against the cushioned comforter while her breasts heaved with each deep breath. The last of her face paint was being rubbed from her cheekbones onto the beige white fabric beneath her. With his free hand, the soldier cupped one buttock to support her and deftly tucked his fingertips into the cleft of her cheeks. He applied pressure with care, just gently teasing, as she continued rocking against his four fingers into her eager pussy and didn't offer any resistance to his probing fingertips circling her puckered bottom.

The Bat's penetration of his cowed villain was far beyond teasing now, and his thickly veined cock was sheathed to the root in the Joker's ass. The pale buttocks clenched tightly, and the humbled criminal mastermind gripped the bat-tool with surprising vigor for one so keen to be caught and punished. A trickle of perspiration seeped from beneath the Batman's mask while the Joker peered at the dark knight with his head turned to look over his shoulder.

The plundered criminal seized his opportunity. "What's the matter? Bat got your tongue?"

The Batman groaned instantly, though whether it was in response to the awful pun or the searing heat of the tight ass squeezing on his cock, Mr. J. would have been hard pressed to call. Almost as hard as the dark knight's police stick had been, the powerful costumed man thrust into the villain's eager body. He'd definitely enjoyed that bit of excessive force. While the hard bat-cock was actually a poor substitute for the unyielding hard thickness that had prepared Joker for more... the muscular grip of firm fingers that wandered from his hip to the flesh of his ass; the sweat of his ultimate conquest dampening his backside... that more than made up for it. The villain had been fucked by better... he'd definitely been fucked by bigger... but he'd never been fucked by quite such a convincing Batman.

Harley had possibly not fucked something bigger. She had pulled at the comforter with clenched fists, kicked until her legs hurt from the effort, and wormed her way across the bed until her head was dangling over the edge. Her soldier never let up, never relented, and she was convinced he was a hired mercenary sent specifically to hunt her down for all her crimes. With practiced skills and a veteran's wisdom, he had spread her sex and plunged so deep that her belly ached every time she tried to laugh and taunt him. Now up to his wrist in her pulsating pussy, her soldier was softly but persistently introducing the fingers of his other hand to her ass, stretching and tugging her pucker open, and creating a feeling of wide-spread fullness that brought happy goosebumps to the back of her neck. She wanted to say something, to demand who paid him to bring her down, but, every time she gasped, his knuckles pressed into the hollow left by her raised diaphragm and established a new and deeper beachhead within her lower abdomen. Robbed of her quick wit and most of her make-up, Harley could only encourage him to keep going with thrusts of her hips and the occasional throaty groan that she wasn't fully aware she was making.

A good soldier, much like a good scout, is always well prepared. If Harley had been more coherent amidst her lust haze, she would still not have been surprised to see that one of her warrior's utility pockets yielded a travel sized bottle of thick and creamy lubricant. If she'd had her eyes open and her head wasn't tipped over the side of the bed, then she might have been shocked by the improvisation that followed though. Removing his fingers from her bottom, he stretched a condom over the broad handle of her mallet, swiped a generous amount of Liquid Silk over the smooth latex while testing the rounded edges of the end of the handle, and nudged the tip of the blunt shaft against the stretched and warmed opening of her vagina. The shaft fit smoothly into the cradle of his palm, following the path opened by his fingers and fist, and fit into place. Harley's eyes shot open as he leaned against the hammer to guide the heel of its handle into her willing body, but, despite the shock triggered by the rigid wooden shaft surging into her sex alongside his entire hand, she made no complaint.

"Around the year 2500, we got really good at improvising." He used his free hand to lift her hips and guide her back toward the center of the bed. The head of her mallet caught, and the wooden handle went deep as she arched her back and groaned happily. "Honestly, the slogan 'Make love, not war' took on new meaning once the sentient machines had tried to cease human reproduction with their artificial intelligence dildos." With a sly smile, he carefully repositioned the hammer handle and tucked his fingers to press the rounded end against her g-spot. "How rough did you say your Mr. J. is?"

Rocked and thrilled by the Batman's pattern of vigorous thrusting and intentionally heavy-handed grip on his hips, the Joker had grown tired of aching and leaking a spreading puddle that ran down to the front of his smart red satin boxers and threatened to cream his purple trousers. He had taken matters into his own hands with his white gloved fingers stroking along his throbbing erection. The ever-taciturn dark knight was near silent now, chasing his own climax in the heat of the villain's tight, clenching ass. Mr. J. built up to a steady rhythm with his hand, slipping precum up and down his throbbing cock and feeling it soak into his glove, while letting himself be jolted through fantasy after fantasy by the muscled man pounding into him from behind.

He didn't need to look back over his shoulder to see the sneer that twisted the masked vigilante's face as the powerful do-gooder hurtled into orgasm. The heat of his release against the latex sheath still flooded the Joker's ass amidst a flurry of staccato sighs and grunts. The criminal mastermind didn't need to hear the wet sounds of the bat-cock withdrawing or feel the uncomfortably cold absence of the throbbing bat-shaft that had erupted within him. It was enough to know that just this time, he'd been caught and punished exactly the way that he'd always imagined. Just this time, the Batman had given in to the Joker's wiles. This time, the vigilante had truly given this nemesis everything that he wanted... and the good, hard fucking certainly hadn't gone amiss. He looked straight down into the comforter, shielding his eyes so the illusion wouldn't be ruined as his Batman started to peel himself out of the muscle suit and mask. He clenched his eyes shut and clung to that last image: his proud Batman naked from the waist down, gleaming, softening and sated, his rippling chest soaking through the grey of his suit and the sneering grin etched on his face. Grinning with lopsided red lipstick smeared on his face, the Joker crushed his pulsating erection while he burned that fantastic image into his mind's eye. He came hard with a choked moan, falling forward into the bed while the handcuffs bit into his wrists, and the strong vigilante stretched out beside him and only needed one hand to lift the Joker's chest to half coax and half drag the villain into position with his painted lips over the shrinking cock between the dark knight's thighs.

"I don't think you've given up your criminal ways yet," the rumbling deep voice taunted.

"What?" was the last thing Mr. J. said before

falling forward into the lap of the naked crime fighter. He obliged, arms trapped underneath his belly, and could only use his mouth to kiss, suckle, and lick the softening cock until it was swelling again and eager for more. Half choking and happily swallowing, his tonsils were quickly soaked with a second blast of slick semen before the Batman lifted him up and turned him onto his back. Apparently satisfied, the vigilante tugged the Joker close and they sunk into a sticky sleep with one of the Batman's heavily muscled arms resting on the devious madman's heaving chest. "I'll remember this next time they tell me nice guys finish last," the Joker muttered to himself. His own cock was throbbing and ignored, and he was certain that there was a lot of therapy in his future.

Despite the intensity of his attentions, Harley was definitely up for the challenge. She laughed when her soldier removed his bruised hand, and only the handle of her hammer was left inside of her pussy. Of course, he expertly caressed and pinched her sweet pearl, making her scream at the top of her lungs while teasing her to higher peaks, and then moved his soaking wet fingers to her bottom. Climbing higher into unchartered euphoric territory as the two and a half inch wide wooded shaft was gracefully rocked into her g-spot, she moaned and whimpered as her warrior's fingers filled her ass and provided the perfect burning counterpoint of sensation to overwhelm her body and mind. He knew women's bodies intimately enough to read all the signs well in advance of the moment, but it was no less of a joy to watch her face contort with surprise before it relaxed totally and she thundered into the rush of her intense orgasm. His fingers, all four, pressed into her ass and her soldier enjoyed how her overworked and overheated pussy frantically clenched hard enough to make her buttocks dimple one last time before her sex's squeezing grip on the rigid handle subsided into soft the tremors of post-orgasnmic spasms. Her puckered bottom pushed him out, and her whole body shuddered while in the throes of an incredibly deep orgasm that seemed to trickle through her until the tremors made one limb tremble after another.

Still in his trousers, the soldier surveyed her feminine form, about to coo the soft reassurances to soothe her reactions to his intense exploration of her body, whisper about his own motivations, and perhaps offer to run them both a nice hot shower. Her fingers deliberately curled so her sharp nails would catch his skin, she slapped him with a laugh. He was caught by surprise when it became immediately obvious that the undone, vulnerable creature of moments ago had disappeared and that Harley Quinn was very much back in control with smeared make-up and a deliciously deviant smirk.

"Funny," aiming a challenging grin directly at her soldier's dark brown eyes. "The future feels a hell of a lot like my last Thursday evening."

"Sexy Identities 5: To Serve The Worthy"
written by Max D

Featuring the Lovers of Sexy Identities

"Sexy Identities 5: To Serve The Worthy" themes: MF, Supernatural & Paranormal, Vampire, Romance, Blood Play, Sitophilia & Food Fetish

"You have no idea who I am, mortal," she murmured with contempt. "You can either do as directed, or the goddesses will sort your bloodless ashes." The tourist made to lift up his camera, still hoping to capture a photo of the ebony vampress, but, with a wave of her hand, he was surrounded by five men in tasteful black suits and dark tinted sunglasses.

With a gesture toward the busy street nearby, and a finger on his earbud, a suit suggested firmly, "Perhaps you'd like to step back and mingle with your own kind." The pug-nosed man pushed his glasses back with a thick finger and made to stare down the row of identical agents, but, from behind him, a broad shouldered man in a charcoal grey suit with turquoise pinstripes smacked into his extended elbow and brushed him aside.

"Ooph. Seriously." The clipped English was aggressive and unfriendly. "You people are in the way." Two of the agents murmured in German, the harsh syllables rumbling with suppressed thunder, and the man gestured straight ahead with his hand. "You can make a space, or you can fall back. Your call." He kept going while the camera wielding tourist stared at his back. "Besides, for a protection detail you seem to have left your lady's flank completely exposed. I wonder how long it will be before she notices?" A burst of radio static came from the earbuds and one of the agents winced. "Yeah, so much for 'this situation is handled.' Did you really think I didn't speak Deutsch?"

The bodyguards parted and then fell in behind the pinstriped suit. The agent in charge was still growling cryptic commands, shifting to terse battle language and abbreviations now that it was apparent that the second guest they were escorting wasn't a typical American businessman. A broad shouldered man with the demeanor of decades of experience, the lead agent was waiting, letting his team pass forward of his position, when the tailored suit finally stepped into the foyer of the convention center. At first, the lead intended to just step in behind the pinstriped suit, but there was something peculiar about him and the agent in charge acted on intuition. His arm lashed out, was blocked instantly with a single gesture of the suit, and then the lead agent stumbled backward from an unexpected blow to his chest.

"You don't want to do that again." The seductive whisper coiled like a cobra in the still air as her red robes flowed over the polished marble of the lobby floor. Both the agent in charge and the pinstriped suit looked toward the venomous hiss of her displeasure, and then the lead agent directed his eyes to the floor and discretely adjusted his suit jacket. "You're the replacement negotiator. How... cunning." Her long fingers stirred the air as she beckoned the businessman to straighten up, but he stayed in a defensive stance while watching the other agents who hadn't moved since the altercation started. "Your employer may not have mentioned-"

"I'm a contractor, Miss. Authorized to do whatever is necessary to ensure a balanced proposal is well received. And your men, after nearly assaulting a blundering idiot in public with surveillance cameras recording them, just attacked me." He rolled his shoulders and neck, his double breasted suit flexing with his compact body, and for a second his shadow seemed to double in size. "I mean no disrespect, but... it is unclear how I should respond to that insult."

Bowing his head, the agent in charge replied, "Our guest is not what he seems." Excuses were unacceptable. Facts were all he had, but, at that moment, there weren't enough facts to explain his actions and express the discomfort in his gut.

Nodding, she understood and took an unnecessarily deep breath which whistled through her teeth when she exhaled. "His spells have been upon us since we arrived. Or did you think it was typical for a busy city to be deserted except for strays and random tourists?" Her arms were lifted, palms toward the heavens, and she slowly turned while gesturing to the empty lobby. "Not a soul. No one at all. Not just illusions or concealment. Just a mage would have been hard enough to find on short notice, but a 'contractor?'" She was facing the compact man: staring him down and studying his physique. "I should be able to read your blood, to listen to the pumping of your heart, and to know the passions that course through your veins. But I can't." She quirked an eyebrow. "Where there should be a soul, there is just darkness. Where there would ordinarily be conflicted purpose, there is just... an endless hall of mirrors. Where there should be the knotted warmth of dreams and desires, there is only rage. And fury." She gestured toward her lead agent, dismissing him with a sweep of her hand, and stepped closer to the negotiator. "I don't even know what you are, but I don't care. If you expected my entire escort to be fooled, that you'd slip by them all without being noticed, then that was your mistake. Besides, you got your chance to show off." Turning her back and heading toward the elevators, her robes hissed across the floor. "We are here to come to an agreement. I will meet you upstairs."

Accompanied by four agents, she watched the man with cold eyes while the stainless steel doors closed. She was certain that as soon as she was gone, he would straighten up, discard the pretense of being offended, and simply take the second elevator. The only possibility that she hadn't considered was how he'd offer his hand to her lead agent - a gesture of respect for sensing the unseeable, and how'd he'd earn her trusted security team's respect by quietly walking forward into the escort of waiting agents. She never anticipated that hidden moment of contact and show of humanity, yet that was precisely the reason why he got results.

In the dimly lit conference room, piles of paper were carefully placed along the dark wood table. He took one look at the refreshments - water, coffee, tea - and asked an anonymous member of staff for someone to fetch sliced fruit and orange juice. She frowned, displeased by such peculiarities, and focused on flipping through the master contract agreement with slender fingers while the negotiator took his seat. There wasn't much to say, but his immediate interest in the contract addendums caught her attention. Together, in their own ways, they set out the facts and conditions relevant to their interests to organize the discussion.

"You first," he insisted gently. He studied her indifference and added, "I have specific requests, but they are secondary to the core binding proposal." His approach seemed clear if a bit too open-handed.

Nodding, she recited six clauses from memory. "Each of these," she added, "unduly restrict our freedom to trade in times of increased need or in situations where you are unable to deliver sufficient supply to meet your quota." He flipped through the main contract and located the clauses with practiced ease. "Do not pretend that you are unaware of this problem. I presume you have an offer to correct it."

"Yes. Along with these clauses, we would like to consider modifying the following," and he recited a short list of other places in the contract restricting supply, "so that you may purchase from any seller under conditions where we anticipate a shortfall or a delivery is lost during transportation." She waited for the catch. "Of course, that waives our liability for such a shortfall or interruption in supply. You will be responsible for making up any deficit on the open market or through other contractual arrangements outside of our purview."

And so, the dance began. Capable of a vast repertoire of maneuvers, the ebony vampress delighted herself by boxing in the cunning beast of a negotiator, and took great pleasure as she defeated his proposals with counter-proposals that increasingly whittled away what little advantage the contract provided to his employers. After a long afternoon, two bowls of fruit and a pitcher of orange juice, he placed his palms on the table and grinned.

"So you are satisfied?" Her lip curled with distaste at the thought of him giving up so easily.

He nodded. "I don't need to be. I've communicated the details, and I've been requested to cease negotiations and see if you will accept the proposal in its current state. I recommended more time, but... some individuals are very shortsighted."

He smiled and winked as if they were friends.

Whatever means he had used to communicate with people outside the room was a violation of the negotiation, but she didn't care. His cute gesture and willingness to write-off his masters' business made him an unlikely ally or a fool. "I am familiar with the entire contract. As soon as our modifications from this afternoon are written up, I will give it my seal." He went to get up, but she tapped the table with her long fingernails to get his attention. "Do you need to leave so soon?"

Settling back into his seat, he smoothed his pinstriped jacket before casting her a curious look. "I would like to wash up. After that, and with this successful negotiation concluded, my time is my own." If she was inviting him to join her then he needed to make sure a suitable boundary existed between one piece of business and another. "I'm sure you have specific interests, but... would you enjoy a stroll along Western Avenue, perhaps down to Victor Steinbrueck Park, to look out over Elliott Bay?"

She considered his offer carefully. Perhaps he was revealing something that she didn't know about him. Perhaps he was luring her into the open where it would be difficult to provide protection and cover would be hard to find. "Will it be crowded?" She preferred to avoid sullying herself in the affairs and pastimes of humans.

He laughed and got up to wash up. With a wink, he replied, "It doesn't have to be." Perhaps the innate distrust of his unnatural state that caused humans to avoid his path and reject his company could be used to woo the reclusive vampress. It was a lovely idea to consider, and he beckoned to the staff and they opened the doors to the conference room.

Expressionless, she watched him turn her back on her. It had all been too easy. Just like the situation in the lobby. As soon as the negotiator was out of earshot, she signaled her lead agent.

"What have you learned?" she hissed in German. This was a setup. It had to be a setup. "And how was he able to communicate with anyone outside of our secured room?" There were no good answers. The agent in charge left out the bruised bones within his forearms and the slashed fabric along his shin and calf. If the compact negotiator had intended to kill him then he would have done it. The use of a hidden and unseen blade was just a reminder to avoid picking fights without sufficient intel to overwhelm an opponent. He conveyed his warnings on a separate channel, and confirmed his orders before giving the command.

The black suited bodyguards were waiting when the negotiator exited the mens room. As one, they fired tasers into his chest and stopped his heart. He didn't struggle - after all, he'd just emptied his bladder in anticipation of their use of overwhelming numbers to take advantage of the situation - though he had hoped for a nice stroll and always preferred to watch the sunset over the bay to drifting within the soul rending darkness of the abyss while his body healed.

"Sexy Identities 5: To Serve The Worthy"

"I shouldn't be surprised," she sighed into his ear as he awoke. "More than a mage. Not human. Maybe immortal? A unique relic of the past." He gestured with his upraised fingers and she handed him his glasses. "Tell me, how exactly does an elemental even have a body?" Her interest flowed over him in dark reds and inky blackness that he could see while transitioning into the living world.

"I don't know..." he adjusted his voice for volume and began re-training his senses to deal with material concerns. "Did we miss the sunset? It's one of the few things that always delights me." The negotiator didn't need to correct her assumptions about his nature. His capture by the vampress was entirely predictable, and she would draw her own conclusions over time while discarding one theory after another. "I'd say you have me at a disadvantage, but, Serafina, I did so want to spend more time alone with you." He paused in the dark, sensing her displeasure, and offered politely, "Lady Serafina? Countess Serafina? Do you still go by 'Serafina di Dio?' I apologize. I am not so good with titles, but I hold you in the highest esteem."

"A lowly creature which understands its presence before an elevated one is no greater for murmured pleasantries." She was angry at herself for assuming that her past was so happily buried. "And how else will you offend me?"

"Did you seal the contract while I rested in the darkness?" Her sharpened nails suddenly grasping his throat made it clear enough that she had. "Ah, yes.

While you negotiated as I had advised you would, the gentlemen who contracted me locked up all but a tenth of global supply. You have released them from any liability for delivery and quantity, while locking them into a pricing structure that would otherwise crush their profit margins. Unfortunately, to do so, you relied on a projected notion of market value, which is now entirely under their control. So you will need to pay whatever they wish for quite some time unless you invest in a competing industry to either create greater supply, which will devalue your own investment, or to develop alternative supplies, which will guarantee a pathway for their business interests once natural supply is exhausted." He had no reason to hold back. She'd killed him once. Killing him a second time would only make their connection more intimate and personal.

Releasing him and sitting in the chair beside his bed, the vampress muttered, "I see." She had signed the contract, but the gentlemen were fools to think that she hadn't infiltrated the highest ranks of their conglomerates and would exert pressure in other ways to guarantee her objectives. "So you believe I am predictable?"

"No." He breathed in the scent of her perfume and marveled at the icy bruises that her fingers had left on his bare flesh. "No, I hope you are most unpredictable."

Her claws made his flesh bleed as she slapped his face. "You are not worthy of any such congress." She took hold of his chest, pressing her fingers into his muscle and bone, and sought out his beating heart. "You will never be!"

His heart was ripped from his body, but he didn't die immediately. "Keep it as a token of my affection, Serafina," he managed to exhale. Then his spirit fled his body once again, and the healing began on its own.

She killed him every night while keeping him locked away from his precious sunset. She never tired of his soft spoken words and anticipation of her destructive urges. He relished it. He egged her on. He all but begged to die from her frozen fury. Though he never said the words, the jaded vampress heard his heart loud and clear... Her collection of his hearts, anyway. One for each evening after that first collected over the course of the lunar month.

It was fascinating really. Just as his body revived itself in the span of a few short hours, the hearts all restarted on their own. They were connected by some invisible force, beating like synchronized drums, and she watched them drifting in liquid filled jars that were placed in a semi-circle around her bed. The dull red of the heart muscle remained untainted by decay despite being kept in a rudimentary saline solution. Each heartbeat soothed her restlessness, focused her rage, and caressed her ears as she slipped into torpor. As the collection grew, her fondness for the whispered drumming of his pulse grew. She awoke from the dreamless darkness to feel her strength renewed and the fire of her intentions kindled by the steady throbbing percussion of his lifeforce. On the first night of the new moon, she sought him out intending to add another heart to her collection, but he was gone.

Fury ignited within her as she stared at the empty bed where he should have been restrained and waiting for her ebony fingers to plunge into his chest. The chase was on. She raged through her household, but the betrayal ran deep and even the taste of her servants' blood did not reveal how he escaped. With global resources at her command, she organized an impressive force of investigators and hunters and set them loose on the world. They tore into mysteries both ancient and terrible, blindly and boldly triggering a red tide of chaos on every continent, but they got no closer to finding the one that she sought. They even began calling him that. "The One," the hunters would whisper, "have you seen him?" The dreaded question sent the weak into hiding and provoked the indignant aggression of the powerful. Vast armies of unlikely allies searched as she stared at his hearts, steadily beating without a care in the world, and her own descent into madness became a spiral of darkness from which she could not escape. After two years of ripping apart the globe for the only creature that she desired, the vampress embraced the pathos of her rage as she squeezed a throbbing heart in her hand and hoped that he felt the crushing force of her displeasure within his chest.

When it continued to beat, unaffected by her icy fingers digging into its flexing muscle, she took it to her kitchens and called upon her most talented staff. That first heart she dined on with pleasure, hoping that the man that eluded her experienced the searing heat of the ovens and the skilled strokes of her chef's

"Sexy Identities 5: To Serve The Worthy"

razor sharp blade. She chewed slowly, unused to eating proper food, and enjoyed the lingering bitterness of brine and stale blood that caressed her tongue. Each swallow immersed him in her darkness. Each jab of her fork pierced his being. Somewhere, she hoped that he was weeping. Sobbing was the proper response for rejecting her dark attentions. Groveling was almost enough for her to consider taking him back.

After the first, she began to have the hearts served for dinner. The second heart was prepared in a wine sauce. She didn't appreciate that much as it drowned the natural flavor. The chef's own blood restored a bit of the proper balance to the heart meat, but maybe she should have chosen someone a bit more refined in their tastes. The third heart was served as a raw tartare, complimented with a hint of onion and squeezed lemon. She enjoyed it immensely. The fourth and fifth... they may have been a bit overcooked, or else his body had been under more strain whilst regrowing them. The heart meat was tough and not appealing. The sixth made up for those. Marinated while still beating in a subtle black pepper and olive oil preparation, the lightly fried and thinly sliced heart meat was exquisite. The next four hearts were prepared in nuanced marinades - dried herbs and a touch of soy sauce being the nicest - though many of the others sadly overwhelmed the flavor of the delicate meat.

A new chef, to replace the second after an unfortunate incident resulting from her displeasure during a disagreement over new preparation methods, decidedly approached the dish quite differently. On a bed of kale that had been soaked in brine, the eleventh heart was delightfully butterflied and aromatic herbs had been rubbed into the pulsating flesh. The twelfth was served after being chilled in a melon soup and then stuffed with sliced strawberries. Thirteen and fourteen benefited from a rosemary mustard reduction and finely chopped potato and carrot respectively.

Honestly, she had never really appreciated food. His heart, and her obsession with it, was an eye opening experience. As she consumed the twentieth, delicately placed on a thin bed of wild rice and seasoned with salted butter and cloves, the vampress realized that there were only nine hearts left. She'd called back her hunters. She'd turned her foolish and expensive expedition into a profitable enterprise by leveraging the knowledge and contacts that she gained by digging into the clandestine regions of the world. Her depravity and insanity were known to those closest to her household, but the staff were all expendable resources, after all. They watched her with cautious eyes always directed toward the floor, but she knew they were betrayers and deceivers of the worst kind. They tried to hide their feelings, but their hearts sang of escape and rebellion. She culled a few, experimenting for the sake of satiating her hunger, but their hearts were bland and flavorless. She would have killed the chef for even serving the crude meat, but he couldn't be blamed for the low quality of humanity's desires.

She needed to procure a supply of something to

take her mind off the coming solitude in her boudoir. She dreaded the day when the last heart was taken from her bedchamber and delivered to the kitchen, but she craved it nonetheless. So she sent out a tersely worded request to the handful of dark souls likely to be able to indulge in her specific need. The responses came back slowly and didn't excite her. The problem was difficult and jaded tastes such as hers would be very challenging to satisfy.

The twenty-fifth heart was memorable - placed in a sealed chamber for a day and smoked with dark cherry wood. It was served while still beating and only lightly warmed to lock in the rich texture of the muscle. The chef had soaked it repeatedly before smoking in a reduced blood broth to remove the saline contamination. It was utterly precious, and she didn't bother asking how many had been sacrificed to provide the necessary flavor for the broth.

To her immense displeasure, the final heart was not memorable at all. Her frustration was so great that the vampress consumed it too quickly to savour the precious flavors of the meat, and regretted each bite more than the last. Her chef made the mistake of beseeching her to slow down, and his blood was rich and had a lovely bouquet which alluded to his own refined tastes when it came to raiding her kitchen's gourmet selections. She almost wished he had been served with the last heart instead of satisfying her rage afterward.

The next afternoon she was waiting, irritated and distracted after a poor evening's rest in her empty bedroom suite, when her black suited escort opened the boardroom doors and ushered in a compact man in a charcoal grey suit with subtle blood red pinstriping. He took his seat without a word, took note of her open distaste for his presence, and smiled. While she chose to avoid even looking his way, he accepted her disdain with ease and began his work. With methodical precision, he rearranged the legal contracts in front of him and paid close attention to the addendums and attachments.

Looking only at his broad hands, the ebony vampress sneered while fanning out the eighteen pages of the main contract across her side of the dark wood table. "Why don't I begin?" she growled a deep voice that matched the polished mahogany. The room echoed with the tapping of her fingers. "It appears that your employer feels I am desperate or otherwise preoccupied. These prices are not acceptable." Her unhappiness scored the top of the table as she sunk her nails into the wood.

His joy whispered of sunsets and distant shores when he replied, "Again, I am just a contractor. Authorized to do whatever is necessary to ensure a balanced proposal is well received." He enjoyed how she froze, her inhuman stillness teasing his latent arousal, and waited for his lovely vampress to look up into his eyes before continuing. "But, I'm afraid, I have other commitments tonight. So when we conclude this negotiation, I will be unable to join you for dinner."

"Sexy Identities 6: Looking for Group"

written by Max D

Featuring the Lovers of Sexy Identities

"Sexy Identities 6: Looking For Group" themes: Cosplay, Female Masturbation, Vaginal & Anal Penetration, Implied MF, Implied Vaginal & Anal Sex, Rubber & Latex & Fetish Wear

The Lone Avenger. I know. There are dozens of Avengers and being a fierce superpowered or heavily tech'd up fighter of evil plots and schemes is hardly something different or new. I always liked that part the best. Just thinking about the long tradition and history that connects me with the past makes me smile. I guess I've always known that I wanted to be something more. I always wanted to run around with a towel flowing from my shoulders like a cape. Now I can dress up and feel the snug curves of my uniform holding me close and reminding me of my higher calling.

Plus, I look damn sexy in form fitting latex. Full bodysuit plus waist cincher that shapes my lower abdomen, shrug with broad shoulders to make me look more impressive, and a line of five bright silver buttons on the neck to make it look sharp, and knee height boots that holster half a dozen false blades as well as my ID, credit cards, and money. I had to add a small clip-on pouch for my cell phone. Ever since I upgraded to a Samsung Galaxy S5, I've struggled finding pockets and holsters big enough to hold it. In uniform, I move with the purpose and pride of someone inspired by duty.

My character's official story is everything that you'd expect. A sudden surge in the presence of powerful aliens and empowered humans resulted in a secret and drastic crackdown led by a newly formed federated Earth government that operates in the shadows behind the official bureaucracies around the world. While unable to prevent alien landings, the deployment of a global surveillance grid made it possible to monitor everyone and the 'Slaughter of the Lions' began. In the end, the only power worth having was evasion and duplicity. Anything else got you killed or launched into the sun. Either way, the 'Age of Humanity' was brutal and by the time it started to collapse with the beginning of the discrete launches of mankind to Mars and other places in the solar system, I was the only one left. The events have been hidden and forgotten, but the surveillance grid is still operating.

Like I said, pretty much a bland bio, but the Lone Avenger isn't flashy. I've been known to wander through throngs of regular humans all day long and go totally unnoticed. When I dress up, when I dare to challenge the authorities with a display of my gloriousness, they still turn a blind eye. I'm so good at hiding in plain sight that the massive databanks constantly monitoring every city and transportation hub just think I'm a goofball. I'd say the same thing really. You'd expect me to, right?

Unfortunately, being the Lone Avenger gets lonely. I mean, even my family doesn't know my true calling. How could I possibly tell them and risk their lives? So I keep going out, hoping to meet that special someone who has the same superpower that I have: hiding in plain sight and totally innocuous at first glance. You know, the sort of person who would be really difficult to actually identify. That's my biggest challenge, but it keeps me going. I visit clubs, and conventions, and anime cinema weekends. I particularly like Helsing just in case you want to send me something on my wishlist! Sometimes I wish my superpower was finding things or even knowing where my car keys went. No such luck.

At least I have a lot of fun looking. Today, I have my latex set out on my queen bed. The slick lube I use to make it easier to slide into my bodysuit is waiting as well. Extra towels to keep the mess to a minimum are stacked by my pillows. I just need a hot shower, shave everything except my long black hair, and then I'll suit up for this evening's adventure. I don't think I'll find him. I've given up on that. Instead, I'll do what the Lone Avenger does best: dress to impress and smile like a madwoman. Also, consume a lot of Jack Daniel's. My secondary superpower.

It's all going great a couple of hours later, the party is roaring along, and then... I stumble into a monster.

~~~

Fetish events are great places to look for someone hiding their powers. Seriously. The combination of lowered surveillance to protect the identities of wealthy patrons, numerous costumes intended to disguise or display various parts of the body, and plenty of facial recognition defeating make-up and masks are just taken for granted. Sure, the surveillance grid sees where you came from, where you go to, but it doesn't always peer deeply into the goings on amongst a bunch of perverse, consenting adults. So I started attending parties about the time I had my latex suit made and was pleased with how well I blended in.

I always blend in so it wasn't exactly a surprise. It's just that, usually, I feel like a pretender on the inside. At most fetish parties, I'm happy. They aren't exactly my kind of people, but they're having a good time, and they all have secrets. So I feel unusually comfortable in fetish parties despite not being particularly interested in naked bodies, public sex, and power plays. The eye candy is good. The passion of the crowd can be intoxicating. I slip through them without being noticed, dance by myself to the tunes I like, and it's just comfortable.

"Sexy Identities 6: Looking For Group"

Until it wasn't. He roared by me, grinning and pouncing onto unseen prey before sweeping his leg out and hurtling back the way he came. The rhythm of the music was racing in his heart, and his body flexed with the pulsing bass. I watched in amazement, my mouth hanging open, as he blatantly grabbed onto something invisible and nullified his momentum to avoid careening into a topless blonde that walked right into his path with no warning. As soon as she passed, he launched into motion and I felt the air twirling around him as he slipped right by me. The song ended, abruptly, and he dropped to his feet at exactly the right moment. Gesturing toward my drink and possibly my latex clad breasts, he smiled. "You look fabulous," his voice resonated with pleasure. "Come out and dance with me... but I have to warn you: I really never learned how to dance with other people."

You know that feeling when you think no one is looking and you discretely tug on your panties so they stop flossing your lips only to look up and see someone staring right at you? Uh huh. No one notices me. That's my superpower. I'm pretty sure I could walk up to the stage naked, and, at exactly that moment, someone would fall from the balcony and everyone would look that way instead of seeing me. I'm never offered a free drink by anyone, and I have to huddle in close to other people ordering drinks at the bar or the bartenders will pass me by for hours without pausing. I'm fairly attractive - I mean, no woman is perfect, but I've got all the right bits and dress up nice - but I used to have a dog so people would at least come up to me to ask to pet my puppy. All my life, I've been invisible yet he saw me.

Confronted with the impossible, I did what any superheroine would do: I fled to the ladies room. I had to push and shove to claim a stall because people kept cutting right in front of me. I had to sit on the toilet with a foot on the door because women kept trying to open it. I had to really work through my emotions because my world had just been turned upside down. It took a lot of courage to brace myself, stiffen my spine, and march right back into the shifting tides of the beautiful, the perverse, and the naked people who didn't know I existed. He was waiting, hopping down from the edge of the stage where he had been perched while finishing a bottle of water, and waved to me.

I went right to him. "And who," I jabbed into his chest and his warmth made my finger tingle, "are you?"

He grinned, gently caught my hand, and softly kissed the pale blue latex of my glove. "Your admirer, of course. Does anything else matter?" He released me, his fingers slipping away, and shrugged. "Would you like a drink? Or a water? You must be warm in a full bodysuit. Don't let yourself get dehydrated. It's no fun the next day."

"Ummm... Jack Daniel's, please." Ok, the novelty of being offered a drink totally won me over. I'd always longed for that, and he didn't have to be half as good looking as he was to charm me with such a simple gesture. "Does 'on the rocks' count as hydrating?"

He even laughed at my terrible joke. "Of course," he smiled, "and I'll get two bottles of water just in case." We waited together at the bar, and I gave him a gentle squeeze every now and again while the bartender poured my drink and he paid for it.

He was real.

And I was in trouble because I didn't have a plan for what to do if I ever found someone like him.

~~~

Can I just say, men are strange? Do I have to describe any more than that? I'll run through the details, part because I want to share and part because I enjoy how they inspire my fantasies, but that doesn't change the basics. He was like a machine. Long after I was tired out and resting while sipping the second bottle of water, he was twisting and cutting across the floor with glee. The DJs varied, but it was generally all electronic mixed music with one or two slower rock songs played for the older attendees. He nailed those, too. It was his passion. The rhythm powered him like winds pressing into a billowing sail, and it was exhausting watching how he tore through the fabric of space just to amuse himself. When he was done, limping and smirking with perspiration running down his face, I was waiting for him to forget that I existed. Like everyone always does. Instead, he slipped in right beside me and closed his eyes while consciously slowing his heart and breathing. I watched him blatantly use superpowers without a care in the world. Anyone could see him. Everyone did see him. He stood out like a sore thumb and couldn't be missed with all his cavorting about.

His fingers were dripping with sweat when he gently caressed by thigh through my skintight latex. "I hope I'm not bothering you." He looked up, his eyes troubled, and I watched emotions slip like storm clouds passing over his eyes despite the brave facade that he was struggling to maintain. "You just feel so familiar. Like we've nearly met a million times and I just keep forgetting." He shook his head while pursing his lips and pursuing an obscure train of thought. "I don't meet many ghosts anymore."

Hello, anxiety attack. I was suddenly trembling like a leaf and unable to say anything. My chest was heaving, and I thought I was going to die. Or my heart would explode and then I would die. I lost control over everything, and I went numb. I wanted to run, but there was no escape. I was trapped in my body, and it was shutting down. Lightheaded with my heart pounding, waves of nausea and dread washed over me and dragged me into the abyss of my own mind. I was floundering in the riptide, and the only thing that I knew for certain was that he was still there. Through the numbness, I could feel him carefully cradling my shoulders and whispering to me. Despite being imprisoned within my body, I could sense the way he was tossing me a lifesaver and encouraging me to take hold of it if I could. He never tried to be forceful. He never tried to rush me. He never called for help or beckoned for other people to come over. I was so terrified that I think I died right then, but when I finally shook it off - still silently sobbing - he was my anchor.

"Let's find you someplace quiet to sit down where no one will bother you." He wasn't asking. With gentle but firm hold of me, he guided me out of the main show room and onto the patio where I could sit in an open space and breathe in the fresh air. He only left my side for a minute though it felt like an eternity. He carried back a second chair in one hand while dragging a small table behind him. "We'll just chill out, and, when you're ready, tell me what you want to do."

He was so one of us. Maybe not an Avenger, but a... something. A couple of women came over to check on me, something that never happens, and he told them that I'd had a bit of a panic attack and asked if they'd bring a cola and a sealed bottle of water. How he guessed from the outside looking in, I don't know. I just couldn't imagine the kindness required to look after me when I was obviously a mess. All from a complete stranger, the only stranger to ever look up and just notice I existed without any prodding or accessories, and that made my heart hurt all over again.

The ladies returned, and he offered them his seat while fetching two more chairs. As soon as he was gone, they asked if he had done something to hurt me or if I thought my drinks had be dosed or if I was taking something that was causing me to have a bad reaction. I muttered that I was just in shock and occasionally get attacks, and they both sympathized and rambled on with stories about friends that they know who suffer from anxiety disorders. He returned with chairs, but the ladies excused themselves instead of sticking around. I guess that I just wasn't interesting enough compared to the big leather clad game that they were hunting.

We sat in silence. Occasionally, he'd squeeze my hand, and I'd weakly squeeze his fingers back. The night passed, and we must have been outside for an hour before they started shutting down the party. I wasn't sure that I could stand up, but I took his offered hand and he helped me to my feet. I stumbled into his chest, and he kissed my cheeks to wipe away my tears. "Don't forget me," he murmured and his breath was warm on my skin. I leaned against his shoulder, and he slowly walked me out to the parking lot. I always take a cab home so I can drink, and he made sure that I had money and knew where I was going before he left my side.

~~~

He never told me his name. He never gave me his number. I pretended for a while that he understood my superpower so he was being discrete. I expected him to turn up at another party. I prepared and planned what I would say - from apologizing for being stricken by anxiety and offering to make it up with a nice dinner someplace. I thought about clothes, had two more latex bodysuits made, and wondered what he was into. I tried to retrace my steps, and ask around about him, but no one seemed to recall him the way I did. I got a bit depressed and honestly wondered if I was just a ghost. That mindfuck lasted for a couple of weeks and then I stubbed my toe on my bedpost and decided no ghost would ever have my sort of problems with clumsy induced agonizing pain! One thing was certain: I remembered him.

I remembered how his fingers caressed my thigh as I slowly stroked my nails over my smooth skin. I remembered the strength in his fingers as he squeezed my hand as I circled my clit with one and then two fingertips. I remembered how easily he cradled my shoulders and walked me slowly to the patio as my caresses slipped lower and tugged at my tender labia. I remembered his powerful biceps as they bulged while he hefted the second chair and dragged the table behind him. My fingers penetrated me with measured strokes that fondly recalled his deliberate strength. I remembered his quiet voice and his offer to do as I asked. I pushed deeper, sliding into my wetness, and I had an answer for him that he couldn't refuse. I remembered his peaceful presence, just being there, and my throbbing grip held my knuckles in place at my opening as my fingertips drifted in the heated passion of my pussy. I remembered his careful questions. He'd ask if I wanted more, and I wouldn't need to say a word. Thighs spreading further apart, a third finger pushing into my sex, I'd make my intentions clear. He'd want to know if I was comfortable going home alone, and I'd tell him to come back with me. Three fingers pushed deep enough to make my toes curls and it was almost perfect. I'd need to undress him, help him out of his latex vest and giggle while unwrapping his black rubber kilt, because it was only fair. Pressing my hand hard against my pelvis and feeling my pinkie pressing into the moist cleft between my buttocks while my other three fingers plunged deep into my clenching pussy, I'd make fun of him wearing a rubber skirt. I'd get a chance to feel up the goods - his goods - and know exactly what I was in for. What the hell... my nail was a little sharp, but my pinkie fit into my tight pucker and penetrated my bottom. Every motion of my forearm moved my fingers inside of my body. What then?

I fully intend to enjoy him like I should have the first time. I'm no ghost. Let him feel my heat as I engulf his rigid shaft within my tight pussy. I'm for real. Let him stroke in and out of me while I hold him close and nuzzle his neck. I'm a superheroine. Let him discover how flexible I am, and maybe, if he can tease me to orgasm, I'll let him try my bottom. It feels good right now, two fingers in my pussy and two between my cheeks. I'm thinking a Spock joke may be necessary, but I'll have to figure out his sense of humour first. I can definitely take it, and he might be the right person to try my limits.

This time I won't send him home alone. This time I won't lose my mind. This time I'll be ready because now I know that he's out there.

The Lone Avenger. I just need to track down someone with the superpower to find him! I need a

"Sexy Identities 6: Looking For Group"

group, dedicated to the cause, and we'll each help one another until everyone has what they need. Whatever they need.

All those surveillance cameras must be good for something.

"Sexy Identities 7: The Griffin's Emissary"

written by Max D

Featuring the Lovers of Sexy Identities

"Sexy Identities 7: The Griffin's Emissary" themes: Mythical Creatures, MF, Oral Sex, Exhibitionism (Vehicle)

While the shaman danced around the beach bonfire to the restless beats of strong hands pounding against animal skins stretched tightly over hollow logs, she slipped from the shadows at the edge of the jungle in a comfortable sarong fashioned of woven palm fronds and soft grasses. Beaded perspiration dripped from the furrowed brows of the dark-skinned drummers as they redoubled their efforts and ignored the white phantom peering out toward their crackling fire. Her feet were muddy and her knees were bruised, but no one seemed to want to look in her direction, or maybe they weren't able to. They were

"Sexy Identities 7: The Griffin's Emissary"

men, though she studied them cautiously just to be certain after seeing so many strange things. Behind her, in the jungle's darkness, large eyes blinked and then the rustling of foliage marked the passing of her special companion. She stepped out into the sharp sawtooth grasses that edged the beach and moved toward the burning driftwood with her hands held palms up in a gesture of peace.

The shaman ceased his dancing and paused when the white ghost reached the fire's edge. He collapsed to the warm sand, leaving a crater where he landed on his buttocks, and muttered something in the local tongue while shaking his hands in front of his face. She imagined that he was admonishing the stars for sending her and clarifying that she didn't look like a Griffin at all. Shaking off his disappointment, he rose again and the drums began hammering into the stillness of the night as his feet resumed slapping against the sand. She listened to the very human sounds of their heavy breathing as the waves broke and rolled onto the beach. She had no idea how long it had been. The shaman passed close by and she breathed in the scent of his acrid sweat and the sharp tang of the briny seawater which had soaked his woven reed loin cloth. Beseeching the heavens to heed his call, he continued his dance and called out with faithful imitations of the jungle sounds to waken the spirits of the island.

The Improbable Woman decided to just enjoy the company such as it was. She doubted the tribe spoke anything even related to the few languages that she knew. The warmth of the fire and the crackling of the burning wood was a treat after the close dampness of Griffin's large treetop lair. To keep warm, their nest was lined with various leaves and rushes from around the island, but it wasn't the same as smoke in her eyes and the sound of drums while blazing orange flames leapt toward her hands and ash flecked her bare feet... This had the familiarity of human endeavours and home. The drummers seemed to be tiring, fatigued from the effort, and she squinted to watch what they would do. It was subtle, the second biggest man nudging the thinner man next to him with his knee while only slightly slowing the regular cadence of his big hands. The biggest amongst them was a small giant, and he used two drums because his palms could not fit side by side on one. He also needed a more effective loin cloth. She carefully leaned to one side because her pussy was still aching from the fevered thrusts of her consort, the magnificent creature that lived hidden in the tropical jungle, and seeing the heavy cock peeking out from beneath the giant's poorly fitted reed skirt reminded her of the similarly sized Griffin's lust.

How had she ended up here? She wasn't sure.

This wasn't her first fantasy. He was just the one that she discovered during her usual daydreaming about Captain Hook and fantastic beasts surviving in the empty places of the world, the forgotten legends and myths trapped within the clandestine folds of reality. Dragons were a daring wet dream, and she adored them for how their quick intelligence demanded acts of seduction to stoke their lust and pierce their wariness. On her back, sliding across hoarded gold coins, she was forced to embrace the pleasure of their scaly cocks while their wicked wings echoed the thrusts of their lust and created glittering vortexes that pirouetted around her. Great rocs preferred to lift her off the ground before slamming her back into their nest while thrusting deeper and deeper. The vast writhing tentacles of legendary sea monsters pinned her arms and legs in place while exploring her pussy, ass, and mouth. Throbbing hell hounds found her willing lust arousing and gushed with heated demonic seed that filled her belly. Her pleasures took so many forms because fantastical creatures were motivated by true lust, without an understanding of the human world and without the base nature of earthly animals. Their depravity was innocent, and she embraced it.

She sighed and tucked the cotton covers of her bed close to her chin. It was difficult working through the emotions that led to this dream. She could rationalize all of it. Her distaste for men forcing... well, forcing anything really. Her reluctance to even consider any act that might harm or distress an animal. She needed something that pushed her further, but what could it be without triggering her defences or breaching her boundaries? Eyes closed, the Improbable Woman knew the truth but couldn't express it fully. Nobody understood.

In the end, it was the dark side that found her first. The monsters that lurk in the shadows at night and can be heard whispering through the eaves just before dawn. The werewolves that have embraced the moon and never revert to human form any longer, yet stand on two feet. The great war bears of the arctic circle, whose counsels hide from human eyes and plot expanding the tundra and vast forests over the ruins of man's cities and farms. They found her through the veil because she allowed one monster into her life, and her lust was such a bright spark in a dimly lit world that all the others flocked to seek her warmth over the bitter cold of the distant stars overhead. Her wolf, if that's what kind of monster he truly was, warmed his cracked and scarred heart at altars erected in tribute to the heat of her passions, and the denizens of the darkness crafted their own temples and gathered their own tributes while hoping to win her favour.

She felt them lurking, the shadows alive with purpose, and the moon gently kissed her feverish brow and welcomed her into the embrace of arousing dreams and eager desires. Griffins and dragons walked those islands, and the drummers said nothing as the white ghost quietly swam with them back to their long boats. With the stars to guide them, the drummers wielded massive oars and skillfully slipped free of the tide's powerful currents near the shore and then headed due north. The weight of the empty sky pressed down on her back, and, somewhere else, the growling night beasts thrust into her quivering sex. Looking ahead into the endless ocean of possibilities, the Improbable Woman imagined great talking birds and rocs, and happily moaned in response to the teasing pleasure of throbbing tendriled cocks threatening to fill her sex with heated seed. The stillness of the ocean appeared as a sheet of glass reflecting the bright stars above, but she sensed the eager tentacles curling below the waves that rocked their boats, waiting to reach up and take hold of her body, and then explore every opening of her body. She smiled and closed her eyes while the oars chopped at the calm water and the powerful men breathed in rhythm with their exertion. She was content, and, in any case, things were much the same though the strong odor of the sea was a very surprising addition to her vivid dreams.

Her tall viking bounded up the stairs and rapped on her door. "Hey, are you ready yet?"

Somehow his eager lilt was at odds with the deep timbre of his voice and hulking frame, less a throwback to his forebears than a man out of his time, leaked through from some saga which might have told of the seductive powers of a wild but soft-hearted heathen witch in commune with sea creatures and other strange beasts. Acquaintances would casually remark how well suited they were, while those who saw more of them were simply happy to see two perfect strangers rekindle a centuries-old love. It was an arrangement of quiet understanding amidst two lives full of mostly enjoyable chaos. He had the car parked outside and, as usual, they really needed to get going in order to be on time for her drumming gig. He returned downstairs and graciously accepted a cup of tea from her mum, and those two made small talk while waiting, which turned into bigger talk because thirty minutes passed before his lovely lady shouted down and asked for help carrying her bags.

He didn't even need to go to the top of the stairs to fetch them, his long arms reached out from midway and he grabbed two suitcases while she gathered up loads of kit and her handbag and came down after him. With a kiss goodbye, she was off in green and red, and her boyfriend was charting courses to avoid traffic and make up for lost time. When they came to a stop at the second light just before the ring road, he lifted his big hand off the steering wheel and caressed her cheek. She'd already fallen asleep again, and her eyes were moving rapidly beneath brightly painted eyelids.

They rowed until dawn, largely journeying in silence with only the sound of the oars striking the water and the water slapping the boats to keep her awake. The men were clearly exhausted, but their muscular bodies moved with automated reflexes and endurance honed by hundreds of similar transits. As dawn rose, the boats gathered close and braided ropes were used to lash them together. Planks were put in place, and the men carefully moved around the ocean-faring platform while retrieving bits of equipment from baskets and pouches. One of them ground powder with dried leaves in a singed wooden bowl and then struck flints against stone until the herbs began smoldering. The men shared the aromatic smoke, breathing deep and passing it around, until it reached her.

She was about to take hold when the shaman shook his head. "This is powerful medicine, haole. You do not take." He lifted the bowl and took a quick breath before passing it back to the men while she stared at him. "Now we are far from Griffin so we may speak." He waited, saw she was not certain what to say, and laughed. "Ah, fine then. We share our catch and then we must rest." He turned and leapt around to the other side of the platform where his men were slowly tying bait onto lengths of fishing nets. "You will see. You will be hungry."

She sat down on the wooden plank, watching the sweating men working with numb fingers, and began to stir, still feeling a dull ache between her inner thighs. She wondered when they would pull off the motorway for a restroom break and possibly some very strong coffee. She hadn't slept well, and, in the rush to get ready, she was certain that something had been forgotten. Coffee with a few sugars would definitely help make a huge difference in how she was feeling. Eyes blinking, she studied the broad shoulders of the Polynesian men as they methodically let out the nets and fastened the fishing line to the boats. They were drifting and the sun was growing warm more quickly than she remembered on the island. She wished that she had thought to bring some long fronds or something to use to both block the sun and fan herself.

"Honey," her viking kissed her cheek, "wake up. We need to get something to eat and then I have to fill the tank and get us back on the road." He took his time, used to how she would drift like this some days, and wondered if she understood how beautiful she looked with her hair slightly mussed and resting on her pale forehead. "Coffee? Some fruit?" His fingers drummed on her arm, and the Improbable

Woman wakened with a start. "Ah, there you are. Come on, let's get something to eat. I'm starving." The urgency in her boyfriend's voice tugged at her, but it was something darker that made her open her eyes and look all around.

For a second, as she opened the car door, she had heard the endless howling of a wolf echoing through fields of vast stone monuments. He was calling to her, and he had seemed so close that she imagined the padding of his heavy paws coming across the parking lot. Instead, it was just a large golden retriever happily escaping the confines of a passenger van and shuffling about on the cracked asphalt while waiting to be walked to a grassy area. She instinctively reached out her hand and let the dog sniff at the back of her fingers before he happily pressed his muzzle into her small palm. "I'm up," she exhaled a bit too sharply and then caught her breath. "Are we..." she looked around again, surveying the ubiquitous scenic nature of yet another services area along the motorway, and sighed.

"Food? Coffee? You must be getting warm in the sun. Let's not get dehydrated before we even arrive." He offered his hand and her petite fingers caressed his palm as she took a couple of shaky steps. Sensing her wobbly legs, he stepped forward and let her wrap her arms around his waist. "Come on, you. Just a short walk and then caffeine! And you need to eat." She held on tight as her viking shortened his gait for her and led them inside.

The shaman watched her slowly chewing the mixture of leaves and berries his men had retrieved from their supplies when the Griffin's lover looked ill and wouldn't accept the raw fish they had caught in their nets. "We will take cover. The sun will steal our strength." She looked around while the platform rocked from the motion of the strong men stowing their fishing gear and bringing out layers of dense netting. They were sluggish after the long night's exertion. Now that their bellies were full, it was increasingly obvious that even moving across the planks and boats was difficult for them to manage.

"I don't understand." The heavy netting was being hooked onto short poles, and those were then fit, and sometimes jammed by clumsy hands, into matching hollow shafts firmly affixed to the planks.

Nodding while taking a berry from her hand, the wizened old man sighed. "It is the way of our people. We must have fresh air on our skin so we can feel the coming storm. We must avoid the sun over the water so we do not lose our strength. We sleep under the leaves of our home islands and imagine that there are trees overhead. We wake in the evening and bathe in the salty tears of the weeping mother. We follow the stars of our silent ancestors to our destination." He nodded solemnly to the men waiting to tug the layered net of woven vines and leaves to their side of the platform. "If you cannot sleep then rest in the boats. That is safest. The sun will be unkind though, and your Griffin will be angry if you are harmed."

"He... he will?" The shaman nodded gravely while getting to his feet and encouraging her to do the same. "But how do you know?"

"You are his emissary. He did not wish to negotiate directly with the dragon lords, kingdoms of the waves, and hosts of the sky." The old man's wiry hands moved and cast shadows onto the smooth planks. "It is lucky that your wolf friend watches over you," he took her hand and guided her to the nearest boat as his men strained to pull the netting snug and into place. "They will respect that. The emissary of the Griffin who is protected by the fangs in the darkness. He chose you well."

His gentle tapping on her shoulder woke her up. She had just been about to slip under the nets, to escape the sun, and then her eyes opened and it was raining so hard that the greens and browns of the hillside seemed submerged beneath murky, grey waves. "Wha?" She closed her mouth and swallowed, lips dry and breasts damp from perspiration, and took a deep breath. "Are we close yet?" She saw the old shaman in her peripheral vision, and blinked several times to focus on her viking where he was seated beside her.

His jaw was tightly clenched, and his knuckles were white as he gripped the steering wheel of small two-door sedan. "You alright? You've been sleeping all morning. Almost had to carry you out from breakfast." He dared to look her way and then snapped his eyes back to the road ahead as red brake-lights lit up in front of them. "Bloody hell, it's like they've all forgotten how to drive because it's raining. It's not like it doesn't do this almost every weekend!" His calm was cracking, and the exasperation in his tone warned of an impending stress-induced explosion.

"Sexy Identities 7: The Griffin's Emissary"

She ran her fingers over his arm, ignoring how he initially tried to shrug her off, and gently stroked the back of his hand. "It's alright. We just have to take it slow and not worry about when we get there. Just getting there safely will be good enough." He was about to object, but her fingers moved to his chest and soothed his pounding heart. "Just focus on your own driving, and let them be. Getting stressed out won't make it any quicker." With a grin, the Improbable Woman whispered, "I bet no one can see into our windows right now..."

"Oh, god, woman..." He let go of the steering wheel with his right hand and gripped his forehead. He pulled on his hair, dragging his strong fingers over his scalp, and then asked quietly, "Do you think we should pull off and wait out the rain?"

Her hand drifted to his waist and then she softly patted his thigh. She snorted a low laugh at his unintentional innuendo, and the lusty sigh that followed with roaming fingers took her viking's mind off the original itinerary for the day and helped him focus on the road. There was no point in him worrying about things outside of his control. The steady beating of the rain on the windshield and murky wet colours of the mid-morning slowly lured her back to other places. She felt her hand slipping from her viking's hip, the warmth of her clothes constricting her motion, and the rocking of the platform woke her with a start.

"No move," muttered one of the men, and he kept a hand on her wrist until he was certain that she understood. The heavy nets overhead blocked out the sun, but the still air was stifling and the water surrounding them seemed agitated and turbulent.

Turning her head, she saw all but the heaviest man drawing wickedly sharp spears from the boats while keeping their bodies hidden under the net. Whatever had bothered them seemed serious and grave, but there was no sign of any life other than their raft when she peeked out toward to sea. She was still looking when a great swell formed before her very eyes, and the shaman was by her side and muttering prayers as choppy waves pushed at their floating platform. Hippocampi erupted from the blue green sea, chomping as their hooves and tails strained while they turned. The braided kelp harnesses fitted to their powerful bodies dragged something heavy from the depths. Rising with a trident in his hand, a lord of the sea seated in his massive white clamshell chariot was soon visible as his carriage breached the surface of the ocean. His hippocampi turned again and he circled the covered platform while coming closer and closer.

She understood her purpose in that moment. The dark monster, calculating and considering tactical and strategic advantages, allowed her intuition to guide their path. Pushing out of the shaman's reach, tumbling adroitly into the nearest boat, she stood and stared into the unwavering murky eyes of the sea lord. "Have you come to speak with me?" His skin was turquoise and blue, and his body lean and sinuous. The wolf disliked the look of his face, and she noted the difficulty in reading the expressions of such an alien countenance but didn't jump to conclusions. "I have not met you before, have I?"

The delicate warble of his voice carried across the water like the song of rain on skin. "I have watched you, Griffin Slave. You journey too far." His steeds switched back and forth as he subtly gestured with his trident. His throne carriage skimmed over the wake of their earlier passage. "Were anything to happen to you..."

Her hackles were up, and dark power surged into her limbs. The Improbable Woman saw the world through a haze of shadows where essence shimmered in various shades of passion, and she discerned the truth of the sea lord's threat. A cold calculating voice whispered in her ear while restraining the fury of the wolf roaring through her limbs, and she listened closely. The rapid distillation of wisdom concerning negotiation and best alternatives to failed diplomacy aligned her compass though it did not change her intentions. "If," she stated clearly, "anything were to happen to me, would you be pleased to meet what lingers in the dark trenches that even you have no power over? If," she focused her voice and felt the patience of her Griffin fill her while the strength of her wolf steadied her self-confidence, "anything were to happen to me, would you gain anything, or simply unite the islands against yourself?" The hippocampi seemed frustrated by their master's tight rein, and the beast lingering on her shoulder grinned at her effective negation of the threat. "I don't think anything will happen to me," she concluded. "We will rest, and then we will row on. Be well, sea lord.

Thank you for showing me your magnificent steeds."

The trident flashed in the bright sunlight, and the ocean calm was shattered by a great churning of hooves and lashing tails as the mighty beasts wheeled and raced toward the deep. Their canted bodies seemed even stranger as they plunged into the sea, and powerful tails propelled them beneath the surface with the mighty clamshell carriage pulled behind them. "I am surprised," the shaman said as the Improbable Woman pulled herself onto the smooth planks and wormed her way toward the shaded interior of their floating platform. "I did not realize." He offered his hand and she accepted his assistance.

"I think he loves me a bit," she muttered and her legs ached from marching. The rain hadn't slowed or stopped, but their troupe still charged the sloping roads and continued drumming with all they had. Red and green on their clothes and faces, strident and very wet pennants and banners leading the way, and she grinned up at her viking as he carried on stoically. He'd enjoyed her touch at the second service stop. The privacy of the foggy windows hadn't been enough to ease his natural nervousness, but her moist kisses and the way her tongue caressed and licked his cock helped. He had tried to hold back, to resist her sexy charms, but her body was full of strange passions and power surged through her sleepy limbs as he climaxed on her chin. Now they marched, side by side, and she laughed at the insanity of her fantasy life.

After this, they'd stay here for night. Their clothes were soaked, but everyone would stay up late at the pub while trying to dry out. She'd collect some hugs and kisses from her ladies, and the usual winks and banter from the men. Then her viking would sweep her away, drive them to their lodging, and, in the dark, his warm body would curl around hers as she moaned with pleasure.

In the dark.

While the monsters stood guard, watching with eyes like distant stars, and seeing through the mortal facade to study thinly veiled purpose and passion. They would form their ranks, organized like constellations, and be thankful for their chance to watch her sensual seduction and her boyfriend's fevered response. Over them all, high above, Orion would look down with his bow at the ready. Perched on his left shoulder, looking out along the path of Bellatrix's blue-white illumination, her personal monster friend would be studying and arraying his forces. The Improbable Woman knew the wolf, had experienced the wolf's passions and soothed his dark fury, but he was something different than the beast whose skin he wore. Something hiding in one guise after another, wearing the forms necessary to achieve his purpose, and shaping a future of possibilities. She saw a glimpse of the real him, just for a moment while plunged into his darkness as he lingered on her shoulder, and now she grasped the importance of his hunger and her lust.

The shaman tapped her shoulder and offered her the last of their berries. It was dark, but the beach fires welcomed the boats. Dull red flames flowed in the distance, and the active volcano at the center of the island grumbled and shook for hours before slumping into broken rest. A keening cry of something able to see them approach echoed overhead, and the rush of massive wings swooping past stirred the ocean's spray, wet the strong men working the oars, and pushed her into the arms of the monster whose shadow was there to catch her. "I see you," she hissed in a low murmur.

"Welcome to the Draco Constellation." The shadows trembled in the distant flickering firelight, and she felt him chuckling against her back. "I haven't been here in ages." There was something hinted at in his reminiscing, some memory of constellations and stars, that nagged at the back of her mind, but she couldn't sort it out. The massive dragon circling overhead smacked hard against the air and the outline of his enormity was clear when he blocked out the stars ahead of their boats on his way to his lair beside the volcano's cauldron. When she looked again, the monster had slipped away to pursue his own secretive missions.

She pushed back the covers, tugging them down, and felt the cool air lick over her exposed skin. It was too hot, and she debated kicking free of the sheets as well while her viking sleepily stroked her smooth belly with his heavy hand. He deserved his rest. She was supposed to keep him company while he was driving them to gigs, but it had been impossible to fight back the recurring drowsiness and vivid dreams. The Improbable Woman kissed her boyfriend and caressed his shoulder while watching him sleep in the dim light. Turning had exposed her back and buttocks, and suddenly the air was a bit too chilly.

Sighing, knowing it was going to be one of those nights when her skin was either too hot or too cold, she tugged a few pillows closer. She experimented with pulling the blankets just high enough to trap her viking's body heat against her chest. He continued sleeping, even when she kissed his lips, and she smiled. He'd get a pleasant reward in the morning for being so patient.

Tucked in close to his long body with her eyes shut, she didn't even notice the tendrils of shadow adjusting the blankets when they fell from her shoulder, and then the darkness slipped away into the night.

"Sexy Identities 8: Anubis And Bast"

written by Max D

Featuring the Lovers of Sexy Identities

"Sexy Identities 8: Anubis And Bast" themes: Cosplay (Anubis, Bast, Nekomimi), Romance, D/s, Submissive Male, Femdom, Strap-On Sex, Anal Penetration, Punishment Play

He did not walk across the streets and into the convention center. He strode with poise and purpose. His golden body paint gleamed in the mid-morning sun, and the hieroglyphs carefully daubed onto his muscular chest flexed with the motion of his body. The golden flail and sekhem-scepter of his office were gripped firmly in his hands, and the knee-length skirt of woven grasses decorated with chains of silver and copper flowed around his well-formed thighs. Even the leather of his sandals had been blackened with detailed etchings, and a single blue lapis scarab was placed perfectly on the narrow strap that slipped between his toes. The dark pigment

"Sexy Identities 8: Anubis And Bast"

applied to his neck was largely concealed by a ceremonial collar that consisted of multiple circlets of hammered metals linked together so rectangular bars formed concentric rings of different colours. No one noticed that so much as the leering of his slightly parted red lips, his attentive and swiveling sharp pointed ears, and the fury within the dark eyes watching the world from within the black jackal mask.

He came alone, seeking others of his kind for the dead are boring company at best. The convention workers carefully draped his badge over one of his ears, and he was not amused. With deft grace for such powerful fingers, he secured the strap to his paddle-like scepter with care so the five rows of carved and painted glyphs were not disturbed. The legacy of his adopted father, Osiris, the sekhem-scepter granted him the power to consecrate offerings, and he held it in his right hand to remind those who might doubt his power to think again. He strode from the growing crowd near the entrance and into the convention center, pleased by the repeated strobing praise of bright camera flashes and cries of surprise. His exit from the Underworld was complete. The sweet perfume that wafted from the oils saturating his bare skin heralded his decision to leave the Necropoli and come amongst the living. He sought to proudly enter the world, to leave behind the mountains and places of solitude where he was relegated to watch and guard the great and the foolish, and with each step he became more real.

His dark eyes were laughing when he stepped onto

the escalator and the machinery of men lifted him
into their false heavens.

~~~

Thunder followed in her wake as Bast snarled at
her entourage. Her lean body was wrapped in a
tightly fitted woven apron with fine gold threading
edged through the papyrus reeds. Her strong arms
were the colour of copper, and flint daggers were
strapped to her forearms to keep her hands free. She
paced her temporary chambers, displeased by the
modern softness of the hotel suite, while her male
attendants tried to soothe her temper. They silently
gestured, helpless in the face of her rage, to invite her
to bathe in fragrant rose water or to partake in
smoked meats and ripe fruits gathered in glass bowls
by the windows overlooking the city. One of them
made the mistake of making a sound, a single syllable
uttered out of habit while repeating an ancient prayer
to Ra in his mind, and she leapt across the double bed
and pounced on him.

Powerful hand gripping his neck, her voice coiled
around them with the dark violence of an apocalyptic
deluge moments before the first lightning strikes.
"Not a word. Not a single prayer. He has abandoned
his post. He has left my daughters and sons
vulnerable. And for what? For his pleasure." She
spat the last word with bitter animosity, and her
servant fell to his knees. She was not the lesser Bastet
of the later dynasties - the domesticated cat-goddess
of Lower and Upper Egypt. She was the Eye of Ra,

"Sexy Identities 8: Anubis And Bast"

defender and protector of the pharaohs, and a hunter of great strength and power. The lioness smiled at her servant's weakness and gestured toward her ceremonial garb. "Bring me my collar and mask. We will go to him and show Anubis the error of his ways." She was a warrior of great prowess, and her mission was clear in her mind: bring that jackal, Anubis, to heel.

A flurry of activity descended upon her as gold and silver arm bands edged with red carnelian and green feldspar stones were wrapped around her sinewy biceps. Her wesekh collar was fashioned with subtle gold tubes arranged vertically between two hammered gold rings. The colours of the inlaid carnelian, turquoise, and blue glass were reflected in the smoothly polished dusky gold, and the natural bronze of her skin appeared rich and deep where the collar rested on her décolletage. Two of her servants prepared her mask, the visage of a pale yellow lioness with deep brown eyes and a red tongue. For a moment, Bast stared into the face of her ancestral nature, grinning, and then gently traced the smooth contours of her spiritual mirror. The soft fur tingled under her fingertips, and she felt connected to the greater whole of herself. "Now," she commanded in a stern whisper while leaning back and letting her fingers drop to her lap. The servants turned the fierce mask around and slipped it onto her head. Leather straps tightened to unite her with her identity, and Bast rose in her full glory, peering out from behind dark glass eyes that flickered with furious awareness.

Silent, she gestured toward the set of three one-day passes in her eldest servant's hand. It was a reminder: they would find Anubis, educate him on the error of his ways, and then bring him home. All in one day so that Bast might rest and feast before returning to the sanctity of her temples along the edges of the vast river valley which she called home. The two servants accompanying her were prepared with leather bags of provisions and currency should any entertainment be required. They took the offered passes and nodded with respect to their elder. Bast led them out of the suite, into the hotel hallway, and they shook reed rattles to mark the passing of the mighty deity down the nondescript passage that led to the future.

~~~

The crowds had swelled like the Nile ready to burst its lush banks, and Anubis patiently paused and posed for another photo. Though lacking the solidity and solemnity of a proper temple, the vast convention center pleased him with its many levels, overlook vistas, and maze of branching corridors leading to seldom discovered rooms. He allowed himself to be swept up by the endless barking cries of enthusiasts hawking their inventions and games. Standing a full head taller than all but the exo-skeleton biomechs wandering the main floor, he attracted plenty of favourable attention. He was readily embraced by groups looking for one more person to join in their fun, and called upon by each trader or entertainer who wanted an eye catching guest for their diversions. On stage, pantomiming the stumbling dance moves

"Sexy Identities 8: Anubis And Bast"

of his newfound companions, he tipped back his head and roared in laughter and the throng of onlookers clapped and cheered. This was nothing like his empty temple, not one bit akin to the somber dim lit chambers of the dead, and he was pleased.

Offered a prize for his performance, Anubis cocked his head to the side and studied the bright colours of the cotton shirt before him. Emblazoned across the chest, the name of the dancing booth's game was edged with bright blue and dark greens. He remembered her, fondly, and scanned the crowd with hopeful eyes. Amongst that cluster of waving and shouting humans or approximations thereof, his dark eyes came to rest on a pretty, blushing kitten with a bright blue wig and red furry ears. Without a word, he stepped down from the platform into the cluster of fandom tributes and strode directly toward her. Her cheeks were fiery red and she was staring at his feet desperately hoping that he would move right by her while the crowd whispered in anticipation of what the mighty deity might do next.

His powerful hand reached down, and he gently lifted her chin with the tip of his golden flail. If he could have winked then perhaps she wouldn't have been shaking so hard as the roar of cheering drowned out her mumbles and the powerful jackal led her to the stage. With a thunderous round of applause, the booth announcer roared, "And the great Anubis has selected his champion! Let's see if we have a shirt for this pretty kitty to wear home tonight!"

Anubis was standing tall and fearless, gazing out

over the convention floor from the stage while the booth organizers hunted for a second t-shirt to fit the petite nekomimi, when he was distracted by a gentle tug on his sekhem-scepter. He looked down into the frightened eyes of his chosen one, her small hand squeezing tight to keep from trembling so hard that she might fall from the raised platform, and he raised his flail high and triumphantly shook it in the air after the younger woman whispered, "Meow," while stroking his fingers.

He sought more moments like that; the roar of such precious life within the convention center stirring within his chest. He walked amongst them - the joyful and the vain and the cheerful and the demented - and he felt like he belonged. The terror and admiration of the adoring catgirls and the nods of acknowledgment from the lady warriors were met with graceful flourishes of his flail and scepter. He strode with purpose, eyes seeing everything at once, and his heart beat with new power and strength. He didn't have a care in the world, for he was free to pursue the pastimes of the coddled, the wealthy, and the foolish. It was exhausting and overwhelming, and he retired to the firm concrete benches that he had passed earlier in the day. As Ra looked down on him, Anubis basked in the sun that filtered through towering glass walls. He was magnificent and his muscles flexed as he tested his strength before idly pondering when he should rise again to seek the praise of his admirers.

Anubis was not prepared for the coming storm though. She was furious and her rage had only grown since being harassed by the onlookers and

"Sexy Identities 8: Anubis And Bast"

photographers desperate to block her passage for just one more glimpse of her glory. Her servants had done their best, but the press of humanity was persistent and unwavering. At the check-in counter, a blue shirt had almost dared to comment on her sacramental flint daggers, but desisted when it was obvious that she would not speak with him except through her servants. The three of them had surveyed the crowd, pestered and harassed by the commoners, while seeking the duplicitous jackal. Only a random lucky chance had sent them this way, to the vast atrium where long queues were waiting to purchase refreshments and food, and she'd almost lost her temper and struck down the dark uniformed mercenary who had disrespectfully fallen into step alongside her and dared to speak to her directly.

Of course, now that his tip concerning where the whereabouts of her wayward jackal had turned out to be both credible and accurate, Bast wished she had kept the warrior to add to her retinue. How he could tell that she was seeking a specific entity amongst the throng of fandom all around them was a mystery that she'd have demanded he answer. She shook the distraction from her mind, certain that she would find him again in his black and blue tail coat with his carefully arrayed weaponry edged by glowing lights, and focused on her opponent. Her servants stood ready as they approached him from behind, and Bast signaled for them to stay back. Her lean body flowed with corded muscle and taut sinew as she stalked her prey, and the lioness minded the pattern of reflections on the tinted glass so the jackal would have no warning. The flashes of cameras and cheers coming from the hungry peasants in their queues to barter for coffee and Subway sandwiches were met with an arrogant wave of his scepter. He thought they were worshipping him. He thought that there could be no other presence worthy of their praise. Her laughter rumbled in the back of her throat and then she pounced on his shoulders, drawing her daggers with practiced ease and placing the flint blades just above his collar and just below his leering jackal mask.

"Should I send you straight back to the graves that you should be guarding... or would you prefer to journey with me to the Underworld and explain your rebellion?" The words were cluttered with resonant syllables and the hum of elongated vowels. Her venom struck him, paralyzing Anubis in place, the stars exploding around them as so many cameras caught the moment of his downfall, and then a sniffled "Mew?" distracted both the lioness and the jackal.

They turned as one, ancient deities more accustomed to the fragrant whispering of temples and the dusty dry air of mausoleums, and stared in awe at the blue-wigged catgirl in her newly won Dance Central t-shirt. Staring at the two perfect Egyptian monsters, she sniffled again and sipped more of her Coca Cola from the sweating Subway cup in her hand. The two menservants came close, uncertain what to do, and Anubis' chest heaved as he loudly sighed. With a nod of his head, his Bast re-cuffed her blades to her forearms and gestured for her attendants to come close. They took their time, knowing the masks would be damaged if handled without care, and removed the heads of Anubis and Bast.

Loudly slurping the last of her drink, the nekomimi shook her head as tears threatened to ruin her perfect eyeliner. "You have a girlfriend already?" She looked ready to run, and then Anubis shook out his bundled dreadlocks and beckoned for her to come close instead. The servants of Bast shook their reed rattles and heralded the coming of the kitten princess, while the lioness smiled and reached out to brush away the tears that stained her rosy cheeks.

"Cousins," the lean warrior responded. "We come every year since my Anubis recovered from throat cancer. I'm afraid he doesn't have much of a voice left." With a gesture, he asked for assistance, and the perfectly attired servants assisted in removing the massive collar that encircled his throat and shoulders. Underneath dark skin paint, the scars and marks of numerous surgeries, feeding ports, and other invasive procedures were obvious. "He was supposed to meet me at the airport, but someone decided to come early to play by himself."

Golden chest puffing out with pride, the man who was formerly Anubis gestured to the pretty young woman. "Totally worth it," he grimaced at the grating sound of his words. "Won t-shirt for her." His eyes gleamed with pleasure and he pointed to his chest while smiling at the catgirl. "Hanif."

Shaking her head so hard that her blue wig fanned out to the sides and her furry red ears threatened to fall off, she replied, "I'm afraid of big kitties." She looked over at the woman who was formerly Bast, and then back at him. "What if she has claws?" She held up her petite hands to show her stubby nails which had been chewed down to dull nubs.

Hanif looked around in amazement. He didn't know what he was supposed to say. This was their third year meeting up and enjoying PAX, and the pretty nekomimi was closest he'd ever come to hooking up with a woman at the convention despite all the ones who wanted photos with him when he was dressed up as Anubis. Could he really be rejected just because his cousin was all fury and sleek power? It didn't even seem possible.

"Oh, that's okay," the lioness laughed at her cousin's confusion. "Lapis," she gestured to her chest. "Like the stone he likes to wear on his toes." She pointed to the blue scarabs on Hanfi's tanned feet and grinned. "See how he feels about me? Good enough to hold his sandals together and cover up where he botched the leather-working because he wouldn't follow my instructions." She snorted and offered her hand. "Men, right?"

A manservant offered to take the catgirl's hand and lead her to his mistress, but the petite woman misunderstood and handed him her empty drink cup. "Coca cola, please," she said politely and the other servant had to bite his hand to keep from cracking up at his friend's open armed gesture of astonishment. "Ichigo... but you can call me 'Clara.' That's me." She squinted at Hanif, studying the contour of his powerful chest and tonguing her lips as her eyes drifted lower and stared at his narrow waist and the fit of his woven skirt. "I like men in skirts a lot." When she turned back to Lapis, her defiant stare was intended to pierce the pretty woman's bronzed skin and shatter her into a million pieces. "But I do not like competition." Hanif and Lapis were both confused by the abrupt mannerisms of the younger woman, and the lean lioness tried to block her when Clara charged forward at her cousin. The agile catgirl ducked under the woman's extended forearm and pounced onto her Anubis' reclining body with a big kiss planted right on his lips. He hesitated, reciprocated, and Lapis turned her head away from the intensifying make-out session with a groan. When Clara lifted away, she wrinkled her nose and gold grease paint coated her palms and fingers as she removed them from Hanif's torso. She stared at her hands, then at her man's broad cheekbones, and giggled. With an eye on the lean woman frowning at her play-acting, Clara carefully wrote "Mine" on Hanif's cheek and added a pawprint while grinning like a maniac.

Shaking his head, Lapis' attendant shook his reed rattle and the ice in the empty soda cup while making his way to the Subway line to buy their new kitty mistress a cola. The other servant came close, and Lapis firmly raked her fingernails over his bare torso before giving him a gentle smack on the bottom, her eyes devouring him before turning back toward their new feline friend "Nice to meet you, Ichigo." Her eyes added the prefix 'crazy' without saying it out loud. "Now, that we're sorted, we'll get your drink, and then I would like to see the convention floor instead of stalking my wayward cousin." She hesitated as the younger woman squinted at her while daubing Hanif's dreadlocks with gold paint. "Is there a problem?"

Sighing happily, the catgirl didn't answer the lioness. Instead she whispered, "She likes to take charge of everything, doesn't she?" to her very handsome Anubis before kissing his ear. When he cleared his throat and went to say something in response, she quietly suggested, "Don't answer that." Her fingers caressed his powerful biceps and she blew him another kiss. "I can teach you lots of new ways to say 'Yes' and 'Yes, please' and maybe 'Yes, more.'" She giggled and gestured for Lapis' submissive manservant to help. "Let's put your collar back on, and you can show me everything."

~~~

Resting as his unicorn companion took a break from the crowd, he defaulted to monitoring the flow of people through the convention center and seeking patterns in their costumes and groupings. Always seeking, always watching, and always assessing the threats of this time, he first heard the reed rattles and then saw mighty Anubis and deadly Bast descending on the two story tall escalators that led to the convention center entrance. He moved without hesitation, hurtling through the crowd with the certainty of a sniper round, and made it to the elevators and to the ground floor just in time.

"Sexy Identities 8: Anubis And Bast"

A pretty kitten was the only person who barred his way as he flanked and then inserted himself into the small group. "Bast," his low voice rumbled as the blue haired nekomimi suddenly wheeled and confronted him, "your passes."

Anubis paused, confused, and looked over the soldier. His strength was coiled around him, the long coat with tails and weapon holsters meant to distract from his compact build and aggressive confidence. In his hands were three sets of day passes for the rest of the weekend.

Irritated by his familiarity, the lioness brushed aside Anubis' pet and was poised to strike. She instinctively checked her blades by flexing her biceps and forearms, but she did not look nor reach for them. Her manservants were unsteady - twice this man had slipped past her manservants and she was reminded of the great leather flail waiting in her hotel suite. "What do you want for them?" Bast growled and her body swayed gracefully while making it clear that she could defend herself.

"Oh... my... goodness..." The blue haired kitten swept the passes from the soldier's hand and looked at them closely. "Now you can both stay all weekend!" She was amazed and excited as she turned and carefully handed one pair of passes to each of Bast's attendants and then held out the last set for her. "Now, Lapis, what do we say when someone gives us a nice gift?" She was grinning at her own boldness and didn't notice Hanfi flinching in terror.

"We forgive the trespasses of those who are trying to be helpful," the soldier replied while shaking his head. He nodded his head to acknowledge Bast's coiled body relaxing, the lowering of her unveiled threat of hostilities diminishing, and smiled. "If your kitten needs adult supervision then let me know. I have a pony girl here somewhere who loves corrupting the innocent and tangling them up in ribbon and bows."

Anubis' hand reached out and he rested it on his precious kitten's shoulder. "Mine," he growled. Despite the atonal distortion of his voice, the jackal's intentions were very clear. Clara turned instantly and rushed into his embrace while kissing his chest. She squeezed Anubis so tight that his body paint left an imprint of his firm abs and powerful chest on her new t-shirt. Whatever she was whispering between kisses was lost on everyone but herself, and Bast sighed and took the passes from the petite woman's hand before they got mussed as well.

Sensing the passing of the moment and filled with the urge to comfort his Mistress, one of the manservants shook his rattle and cleared the throng with a sweeping motion of his arms. The other joined him. They began chanting in low sonorous tones, prayers for the dead and the great gods and goddesses, and the soldier faded into the sudden crowd of photographers before vanishing. Only Bast's keen eyes tracked him back to the elevator, and she looked up to see a pretty woman looking over the railing two stories above and waving for the soldier to return to her. "He has companions," she murmured to herself while visibly checking her blades and walking past the disgraceful behaviour of Anubis and his precocious pet kitten.

Clara would not allow anything to separate her from Hanfi. She stayed close to his side, his strong hand in hers, and nervously looked around when Lapis made it clear that her hotel suite was right next door and close enough to hear them if they didn't keep the noise down. She knew that the powerful woman was baffled and uneasy after the strange glowing man had slipped them weekend passes. She understood all about women who needed to control everything and always have their way. Eyes rolling and nose twitching in the manga version of the scene, Clara pushed Hanfi to the bed and did her best to remove his jackal mask before finally calling out for help. A manservant arrived, muttering apologies, and undid the straps with care while gently swatting at her hands whenever she tried to help. Then he left, shaking his head, and returned to his Mistress' suite.

With a nervous smile, Hanfi tugged a pad of paper and pen over and wrote, "We need to wash off the body paint. I think your shirt is ruined." He waited for her to read his words, and then struggled with why Clara just sat watching him.

Taking the pen away, she responded in looping cursive, "You just want to get me undressed. ^.^ Maybe if you say please..." Her satisfied grin at his wide-eyed alarm summed up her pleasure.

Hand shaking, Anubis started to write. He got as far as "Ple" before Clara covered the pad with her fingers.

"Can you ask?" she looked at him hopefully. "Does it hurt?" Her fingers stroked over his muscular forearm. "I heard you before."

His damaged vocal chords produced an uneven breathiness as the timbre of his voice cycled up and down. "Clara... I sound terrible." She blew him a kiss. "Do you want... to wash up... together?" He had to pause to breathe in, unable to steady his tonality but trying hard to relax like his speech therapists had coached him despite how anxious he felt.

"I thought you'd never ask," she caressed his collar. "Help me undress you so I don't have to call out for a servant again." He froze and she giggled. "I just wanted to know if they were really eavesdropping."

They both laughed when there was a soft banging on the wall. "She's very... protective." Hanfi shrugged with his shoulders and hands. "Still in trouble... for slipping away." He let Clara slide into his lap, perching on his strong thighs as he sat cross-legged on the bed, and Hanfi whispered, "It's been... a long time." Her hands stroked his bare chest, and she explored the edges of his Egyptian collar.

"So what will you wear tomorrow?" she sort of understood how the clasps worked, and her nimble fingers carefully undid them. "Are you always a super sexy god?"

"The afterlife..." he whispered to her cheek, "it's

"Sexy Identities 8: Anubis And Bast"

my thing." The collar came away, and he waited for the dreaded moment when Clara would press into his scars and the deadened nerve endings would reduce her touch to that of a ghost. Eyes shut, he gasped and coughed when her hands found his firm manhood through his skirt instead.

Giggling while repositioning herself, Clara fought the urge to make sure her red cat ears were still in place while caressing his ample erection. "I think this is your thing, actually." He opened his eyes, and she smiled so hard that her cheeks hurt. It was hard to be certain, but Clara suspected that her Anubis was blushing. "Will you weigh my heart?" She reached down and guided his shaky hands to her breasts. "Don't worry about getting paint on my t-shirt. It's probably ruined."

In awe of her intense flirting, he cradled and cupped her soft curves while trying to breathe. "How did you know?" He had a fetish for women's breasts, but he'd been on his best behaviour because his cousin had pointed out repeatedly that ogling the massive tits that were barely covered by costumes reduced him to just another horny guy no matter what outfit he was wearing. Granted, the jackal mask did allow for discretely staring at whatever caught his fancy. It also made it very hard to see at all.

Stroking his thighs and seeking the proof of his lust for her, Clara replied, "Oh, archaeology major for two years before changing to philosophy." She found his manhood and gave him a light squeeze. "The 'Weighing of the Heart' ritual always seemed so romantic. Of course, literally putting a heart on a scale is kind of gruesome." She pressed her lips to ear and whispered, "My nipples are very sensitive. Be gentle with your fingers, please. They prefer kisses." The giggling kitty act was set aside for more important things. "Do you like gruesome? We could go as zombies tomorrow since there's a Walking Dead flash mob planned. And there's a nerdcore party tonight, but I'm always too shy to go alone. Plus..."

He gave her arm a firm squeeze. "I'm here... all weekend," Hanfi sighed.

"Right," Clara said happily, "so back to undressing." She winked and stole a kiss from his lips. "No teeth, please. Though I do want your mouth on every part of me." Exhaling with pleasure, his pretty kitty giggled. "I could be a zombie kitty and you could be Anubis again, and everyone would know you were my escort to the Underworld and that would be so cool." Her gleeful gushing finally made sense as he stroked her cheek with his finger.

"I'm more nervous... than you are." He kissed her lips, and then they both jumped as a dull banging on the wall interrupted them.

Roaring so she'd be heard while cackling madly, Lapis shouted, "Get a room!" Hanfi and his kitten were being far too quiet to be trusted. Her manservants were stripped down to their linen briefs, and she delivered another series of lashings with the leather flail while they dutifully held still. The marks of her fury were visible on their bare skin, and they dared not move while bent over the double bed. "Which one of you," Lapis hissed, "deserves my special strap-on?" Neither volunteered. "Both of you then. How wonderfully special for me." Her arm was tired from wielding the heavy flail, and she was craving their pitiful cries for mercy while seated on her stone phallus.

Clara muttered something under her breath while Hanfi just laughed. "She can't... hear anything. She's just... fussing... at us." He hugged her close. "Where... are you... from?"

Shaking her head and finally forced to check and adjust her ears when they tugged on her blue wig, Clara replied, "I want you naked first. I don't want to be sad. What if you live too far away for me to visit? I don't want to think about it." Her hands pushed on his chest and Hanfi let her shove him into the pillows. "You don't live too far away, do you?"

"I'm retired," he exhaled softly. "Work as... a cemetery... caretaker..." Her eyes lit up, and Hanfi was amazed that his delightfully educated kitten wasn't put off by his limited career. "American Legion... Granite Falls." He swallowed, worried that he'd disappointed her, because Clara was clearly lost in thought with her eyes squeezed shut.

Picturing the best route, she concluded that he'd have to drive. "I live in West Lake Stevens. You can pick me up. The bus takes ages." He seemed nervous again, and Clara grinned when she opened her eyes and saw him biting his lower lip. "Are you sure you want to see me without my wig and ears on?"

He was ashamed to ask, but it was a fantasy that had kept him going to PAX year after year. "Can you be... a kitty... with me?"

His shyness was adorable. "Mmmhmmm... so undress you... undress me... wash up... and..." She kissed his cheek and leaned into his firm body, "Of course, I'll wear my kitty ears for my gorgeous Anubis." Her hands felt up his hard muscles. "Maybe you can get me a tail, too?" He tried to hide his eager smile, but Clara's intuition told her they were a perfect match. Unlike his fierce lioness cousin, she was a kitty who loved to weave between legs and curl up in the sun and be a nuisance when she didn't get enough attention and petting. Her fingers found his and she contentedly sighed, "All mine."

They were in the shower so they didn't hear Lapis' triumphant war cries. Her manservants cowered with excited terror as her strong hands firmly guided one into her lap, her strap-on finding its mark and making him tremble as he slid down the stone shaft, while the other gave her a much needed massage. The lioness would have been disappointed to know that she wasn't interrupting her cousin's shy lovemaking with her overt debauchery, but she was too happy to care at the moment. With a full weekend of PAX ahead of her, she considered the possibility of finding the future warrior and his pretty companion to show her thanks. Thrusting hard into her attendant, basking in his pleading for more gentle treatment, the lioness was already plotting the path of her hunt through the convention center to seek her prey.

"Sexy Identities 9: Living The Eighties"

written by Max D

Featuring the Lovers of Sexy Identities

"Sexy Identities 9: Living The Eighties" themes: Crossdress, MF, FF, Romance

Duran Duran whispered from the speakers, lost in a trance of looking all around hoping to find a sign of life in the great beyond. Teasing his big hair, and pulling out a massive can of Aqua Net to guarantee it would stay that way, he smiled while his lips murmured half formed syllables and his soft tenor voice drifted along with the melodic words. His painted nails toyed with a stray curl collapsing to his cheek, and everything was almost perfect. He just needed to shimmy into his beige pant suit, quickly iron his bright red blazer and make sure the pads under the enormous shoulders were just right, and then it would be time to meet the men.

Once the hairspray dried anyway. It always went on wet and sticky and then everything was in that tacky stage for so long. Nathan was just glad that his nails had dried so fast. He'd only made one minor mistake, a bit of cuticle on his left pinkie was suspiciously blackened, and a q-tip with a touch of remover was just the thing to fix that. He tugged out what he needed and was very cautious, remembering the last time he tried to wipe off a bit of bright blue nail polish from the side of his thumb and ended up giving up and redoing everything.

His make-up mirror reflected the mess behind him as he looked down and focused on his nails. On the bed were the five outfits that he had considered for this week's eighties night. The beige pant suit had been an obvious choice when Nathan considered the shabby state of his lower legs. His favorite red dress was right out thanks to a shaving incident that had left a long, prominent scab on his left shin. Not that anyone seemed to understand his fascination with Madonna's "Who's That Girl" phase, but he had immediately fallen in love with the poofy ruffles the moment he'd passed the boutique window display. Plus, it added volume to his slender hips which made him feel wonderfully curvy. The whole look - with matching red waist cincher and sequined cones for his breasts - was ruined by the scandalous slip of his razor. In fact, that painful result of a rushed frenzy to prepare for a possible date had nearly ruined his life because Nathan's fabulous Marilyn Monroe dress was right out, too. So, admittedly the pant suit had been a compromise - though a superior choice to his denim farmer overalls or black Robert Palmer suit.

He was just about happy with how his fingernail looked when the q-tip squished a little and nail polish remover wet the entire side of his finger. Acetone. It was the bane of his existence! Checking the time on his faithful digital alarm clock, it was obvious that his nails would need to be touched up later. Happily woozy from the hair spray and polish remover fumes, he checked his enormous hair, stood up from his make-up vanity, and discretely blotted his pinkie nail on a cotton swab before heading into the bathroom for a quick release. The men wouldn't possibly outdo him this week.

Of course, the men - Jennifer and Susan - aimed to prove Nathan wrong this week like every time they met up at the eighties night. Tonight would be "Hungry Like The Wolf." That was their thing: selecting a song and then charging around all weekend to find the perfect outfit to go with their theme. Jennifer had found the perfect casual safari outfit, complete with loose fitting tan linen jacket, white linen trousers, and brown brimmed hat with a tan band. She was borrowing Susan's sunglasses with the classic leather blinders on the sides, and had spent the last half hour making sure her tight elastic banding flattened her breasts so she could go out with the V-neck of her polo shirt hanging open like in the Duran Duran video. Susan felt a bit put out, but she went tan trousers with white jacket and a beige-tan snug fitting t-shirt beneath. She'd tried for the headband look, but no matter how she rolled and

"Sexy Identities 9: Living The Eighties"

folded her red bandanna, it just wouldn't stay in place without mussing her fussy short hair.

That was ok, though. Susan had a secret edge that would definitely leave Jennifer fuming all the way to the club. Right before they headed out the door as Jeff and Sam, Susan ducked into the bathroom. Jennifer was complaining about being made late by last minute nerves, and was too agitated to even notice what her partner had done before they were in the car and on their way. When Jennifer now Jeff noticed, she screeched and hammered the steering wheel with mock fury. "Why didn't I think of that?!" she roared and then shook her head while pursing her thin lips. They drove the rest of the way in silence, Susan now Sam gloating over her perfect imitation of claw marks on the left side her face that started at her jaw and continued down her neck.

The bouncer made a cursory scan of their IDs and waved them in. They were regulars, out almost every week, and the big man quietly let them know, "Natalie just arrived." With a deadly serious look, Sam winked at him and stalked into the club like Elmer Fudd sneaking up on a wascally wabbit. The drifting pop melodies of the past wafted toward them as soon as they were through the doors.

"Stop playing," Jeff swatted Sam's hand. "I love this song. Love it!" They trotted up the stairs, burst into the faux disco lights, and charged onto the dance floor as "Chains of Love" embraced them with symphonic moments that lasted forever. Natalie was there, pulling off a very credible Dixie Carter circa

"Designing Women" with teased hair, big jacket, and glamorous make-up. Her jet black nails, looking a bit uneven as always, were Natalie's only concession to her enduring romantic lust for Andrew Eldritch of Sisters of Mercy, though Jeff and Sam knew she really had hoped to grow up and become Andrew because Natalie was all about the ladies in the bedroom. Something the three of them definitely shared in common.

"There you are!" shouted Natalie while fast stepping on the dance floor. "I thought you'd forgotten." She winked, batting her luscious lashes because it felt fun despite the lighting being too ambiguous to properly show them off, and went back to doing something akin to a fast foxtrot. Sam joined in immediately, and the two of them were rocking in no time. Erasure naturally led to Depeche Mode, and "Fly On The Windscreen" settled it for Jeff. He needed the hard stuff if the DJ was hellbent on diving right into the brutal tracks of the mid-eighties.

Jeff excused himself, aiming to source one stiff gin and tonic before he would dance to anything, and made his way to the bar. From there, he watched his cavorting friends while tipping his hat to any attractive ladies that looked his way. His short nails didn't completely disguise the femininity of his slender fingers, but he wore all the right accessories. His over-sized TAG Heuer watch had been custom fitted to his slender wrist, and the polished steel and bright blue highlights matched his belt buckle. He'd worn distressed brown leather boots to match his safari look, and a shark tooth on a flat braided leather cord hung loosely around his neck. The Duran

"Sexy Identities 9: Living The Eighties"

Duran video had a specific necklace - maybe a scorpion or something - but it was impossible to tell in the grainy YouTube upload. There had been a big fight when they couldn't find the original videos which Sam swore had been unpacked when they moved into the new flat. Jeff suspected it was still in the box of stuff in the attic, but whatever.

On the edge of the dance floor, weaving between the structural pillars that usually separated the partying crowd from the onlookers, a compact man and a very busty redhead were tearing things up. A handful of smaller asian women had come close enough to be nearby, but only one of them actively played with the hardcore dancers. She was petite, lean, and beautiful - not normally Jeff's type since he adored Sam's long legs and broad shoulders - and there was something sweet about the way the bigger man would pause for just a second to catch the petite woman when she seemed to flounder on wobbly legs. The redhead... wow! Totally the sort of woman that Natalie would be all about, but she seemed to be indifferent or irritated. So many women just didn't understand how resting bitch face set everyone's expectations. With a sigh, Jeff slammed back the rest of his drink and ordered a second. And a bottle of water with a straw for Sam and Natalie. Those two would dance for an hour before they realised that they were dying from thirst.

In the center of the floor, Natalie turned and laughed while Sam raised his hands and shouted along to "I Just Died In Your Arms Tonight." A pretty blonde in black lace and flowing skirts kicked and spun nearby, and the press of the young twenty-somethings was palpable as they tried to crowd into the limelight. Surrounded by shuffling men and women, leaning and gesturing with their hands like so many dressed up mannequins pressing close to the storefront window, Natalie closed her eyes and wished for the quiet kisses of Tiffany whispering "I think we're alone now" while her jean jacket opened up to offer some place to rest under the twinkling stars. Sam's strong fingers gave Natalie's arm a squeeze, and it was an effort to blink back the tears so her mascara wouldn't run and leave inky streaks on her cheeks.

Jeff was laughing. "Got a fake lash in your eye?" he offered the bottle of water, already opened with a straw sticking out of the top, and leaned in close. "Pull it together, silly. You've got an admirer." Natalie gratefully sipped the cool water, smudging the straw with bright red lipstick, and allowed Jeff to subtly steer their happy trio to the right.

There she was with subdued make-up and a perfect black sweater dress. The soft dimples and powerful jawline of Belinda Carlisle lured him in, just like when she recorded "Mad About You." Nathan remembered having the perfect Rick Springfield feathered haircut back then in hopes of landing a beauty just like the pop star. Lost in her eyes, pushing Sam's hand away as he tried to prevent Natalie from staring, he stumbled forward on his high heels and did a sexy shimmy that probably came across as a drunken bounce with far too much shoulder action while approaching the pretty brunette.

"Sexy Identities 9: Living The Eighties"

"Oh, hey," she said sweetly while looking up at Natalie's soft lips. Her hand slipped into the big red jacket and stroked over Natalie's ribs. "I always hoped you'd finally notice me." Her eyes were shut, and it didn't matter that the DJ was playing "Walk Like An Egyptian" because Natalie wasn't going to do anything that might make the pretty woman let go.

Pointing and posing, Sam politely tugged on Jeff and whispered, "Stop staring and start dancing, you lush." He didn't approve of hard alcohol, but Jeff always insisted on a few drinks to take the edge off. When they first started dating, Sam had worried the drinking was all about being cross-dressed in public. Sam was concerned that Jeff was just pretending and the slender woman was put off by Sam's behaviour. Now she was certain it was a bit of crowd anxiety. Still, shifting to just beer seemed a better way to go. Besides, the lingering bitterness of the gin was very unpleasant to taste on Jeff's tongue.

A cluster of cheering small people stumbled backward into Sam's legs and derailed his train of thought. Jeff whirled as a strong arm shot out and barely caught a very drunk dancer before the lean asian woman fell on her ass. "Hey, watch where you're going..." Jeff stared into the dark eyes of the compact man from earlier and took a step closer to Sam as the lean woman flailed a bit while dancing to something only she could hear in her inebriated state. Looking through the round lenses of the man's glasses, staring into the depths of his serious brown eyes, Jeff saw a flame burning bright and decided it was best left to singe someone else. "Let's go someplace a bit less crowded," he murmured to Sam and slowly guided them out of the press at the center of the floor.

"We all fall in lust in the darkness, alone, and then the object of our affection... is just a representation of what we crave to become," she whispered to Natalie while holding her close. "Do you understand?" She took Natalie's nod to be an affirmative, and gently kissed her chest. He was right there, hidden within the glamour of everything he had ever wanted to have, and she understood completely. What woman didn't want to look like her idols? What was wrong with a man who loved those women so much that he wanted to be as beautiful as they were?

Nathan wasn't entirely listening. The attractive woman had her arms wrapped around him and her words were muffled as she spoke to his chest. He'd always been a little too tall, a little too slender, but she fit him just right. He wanted to hear what she was saying, he strained to make out the words, but, between the dizzying internal debate on what should he do with his hands and the speakers belting out "Come On Eileen" all around him, all Nathan knew was that her words were like soft kisses to his satin pant suit blouse.

She was in a poetic mood brought on by happy coincidence. "Because you're hunting, you're getting lost in the pursuit, you're racing along, plotting and outwitting your prey, and the high makes it impossible to not think about everything and anything that you will do as you sink your claws into tender

flesh and bite down hard on what you've wanted..."
With a tender nip, her teeth grazed his pecs and she
inhaled his flowery perfume - the same scent that
she'd worn when she was younger. "You're
vulnerable. Half blinded by your own need. The
mouse only needs to lead you into the dark places
where it has the advantage, where your swords cannot
be swung and your dagger cannot be tugged from its
sheath. You're a predator undone by everything that
you've always needed." She pressed her body against
his, feeling the disguised lump of his manhood
rubbing against her belly, and grinned. "You're
vulnerable, and vulnerability makes it even harder to
resist. You want to burn and rise again like the
phoenix, to feel the trap spring shut and fight against
it with everything... to prove that you can win, will
win, and take what you want." Her fingernails sunk
into his smooth back, and she held on tight while
swaying against his body.

He heard that little bit. "Take me," he pleaded to
the highlights in her dark hair. Her warmth stirred up
passions and sentiment that he thought had been
buried and suppressed by countless nights of
loneliness punctuated with singular moments of
frustrated sex. "I won't stop you ever." She was
exactly what Nathan needed - what Natalie had
always hoped to discover - and her tight hold on him
was all about acceptance without asking any
questions.

Sam and Jeff delicately interrupted their intimate
union. "I brought you another water," Jeff sang over

the rolling thunder of an impending Def Leppard track. "I don't think we've met," he offered his hand to Natalie's admirer.

She looked up, hungry and distracted, and it took a moment for her eyes to focus. "Oh," she rested her cheek on Nathan's blouse and peeked out of the big red blazer, "I didn't recognize you, Jennifer." Looking up, she sighed, "We work in the same building downtown. Small world, I guess." Jeff looked mortified, but Sam was laughing. "What?"

"You're Aimee! I see you at Starbucks when I have to run an emergency double espresso upstairs after hours to a certain work-a-holic." Sam was highly amused, but didn't share why. Natalie and Jeff just stared him down, but it was apparently a secret. "Well, now that I know our good friend is in beautiful hands, I guess we'll let you be alone for a while." He took hold of Jeff by the jacket sleeve and promptly dragged him away.

"What was that all about?" Natalie asked nervously. She felt emotionally exposed, and Sam's laughter made it clear that she knew nothing about the woman in her arms. "Are you making fun of me?"

Aimee shook her head. "I asked about you. Wanted to meet you. Susan said that you weren't my type, but she was so wrong." She reluctantly slipped out from under Natalie's jacket and smiled. "Want to come back to my place?" She sensed the tall man's hesitation and rolled her eyes. "After they play something gothy enough for you," and Aimee lifted his hand and kissed his black fingernails.

"Ok," Natalie stammered while blushing. "I mean... definitely." He was rescued by Tears For Fears, and, together, they belted out the lyrics to "Everybody Wants To Rule The World" while Aimee held his hand and he danced in his high heels while trying to avoid squeezing her petite fingers. Their world became smaller, the lights and sound curving around just the two of them, and nothing else could have made him happier.

Duran Duran was clearly an understated look for the evening. No one even seemed to notice. Except one man, and he was blocky and square cut with a clippered goatee and mustache that suited the hard edges of his face. "Sorry about that," he offered his hand to Jeff by way of apology for earlier. "I've never seen my friends out with their extended family, and apparently it involves a hell of a lot of alcohol." He gestured toward Sam when Jeff didn't take his hand. "I like the safari theme this week. A few weeks back... I think it was trenchcoats and gangster suits... or was that the month before?" He was trying to be gracious, but Jeff just wanted the dancer to go away and return to his busty redhead and the petite asian who kept stumbling into everyone.

Sam stepped in as he always did and smoothed over the rough edges. "Don't worry about it. Every week is a new thing. We're just keeping an eye on our friend. She's got more action than she may be able to handle." He pointed toward the affectionate couple, but the older man was already looking at Natalie and

Aimee.

"Yeah, she used to hang out in the Starbucks when I worked in one of the towers in Reston. Nice dresser, very professional, but almost always off in her own world reading a book of poetry. Pretty rare and absolutely adorable. Haven't seen her in a few years though." His comments registered with Jeff, and sharp eyes looked him over thoroughly. "Finally recognized me. Pierced my super secret disguise so quickly." He laughed and grinned. "I always look like me."

Jeff nodded. "You're the self-important guy busy telling everyone what to do and then jets off to someplace else to screw things up. Totally recognize you." He scowled at the bright eyes and grin. "So where are you off to next?"

"Oh, nowhere. After my team spent nine weeks sorting out two years of installation and configuration mistakes made by your colleagues' subcontractors, I'm quite happily working from home for a few months for clients that don't want to pay for travel costs. So I can come out dancing, entertain myself, and maybe get some extra hugs with my ladies."

Pouncing on that, Sam volunteered, "The redhead? She looks amazing." Almost on cue the curvy woman approached from the ladies room, but right on her heels was the black lace and fluffed skirts blonde that had been aggressively dancing close to the center of the floor most of the night. "Ooooo..." Sam murmured, "why can't I have nice things?"

"Sexy Identities 9: Living The Eighties"

Jeff elbowed his companion hard enough in the ribs to make her yelp and mutter about bony bits best kept covered up. The consultant laughed and took his ladies to the bar for drinks. Hissing just loud enough to make his threat clear, Jeff stopped Sam's attempt to follow the trio. "You will not pursue crazy goth women. What would Natalie think?" Sam laughed and pivoted, diving in to plant a kiss on her lover's lips. "You will also," Jeff was interrupted by another kiss, "not put a poster sized print of that gorgeous blonde on our ceiling over our bed."

Rubbing his nose against Jeff's forehead while delicately kissing his eyes, Sam whispered, "But you can't stop me from imagining it's there..." He suffered his lover's slender fingers poking at his belly while swaying along to Huey Lewis And The News bemoaning their need for a new drug before the flood of designer drugs changed everything in the nineties.

After a long stretch of a playlist straight off MTV PostModern - Depeche Mode, New Order, The Cure, They Might Be Giants, and Siouxsie and The Banshees - Natalie was exhausted and Aimee had already kicked off her wedges. Things slowed down with "We Didn't Start The Fire," and they held hands wandering to the bar while Billy Joel just couldn't take it anymore. David Bowie was a surprise follower, most likely a request, and Aimee pawed at Natalie's chest for a peck on the lips that left a ruby red stain on her cheek. "Oh, baby, just you shut your mouth," Aimee whispered in a deadpan imitation of Bowie when Natalie started to fuss about the lipstick, and they laughed while hugging each other close.

"I should go," Natalie kissed to Aimee's forehead. "I've got work in the morning."

The woman wrapped her arms around his waist and squeezed him tight. "No. You should go with me. We should go." Aimee tried to work her brain around what she was trying to say. "Let's go together." That was close enough.

Unable to make out the words, but understanding the intentions, Natalie moved with Aimee and they fetched her wedges from behind the speakers before heading for the door. Sam and Jeff waved from the corner where they had not so discretely been making out. The glaring brightness of the streetlights brought on the moment of truth, and Nathan who was Natalie looked down at pretty Aimee waiting to be rejected for his imperfect make-up and manly hands and the ridiculous pant suit that had not been very flattering at all.

Aimee just wrinkled her nose, flashed a smile that put Belinda Carlisle to shame, and tapped his nose with a slender finger. "Poof. Just you and me." He didn't need to look around to know it was true. No one else mattered anyway.

The soft murmur of Duran Duran played in his head as Nathan invited Aimee under his big red blazer and they walked to his car.

"Sexy Identities 9: Living The Eighties"

"Look now, look all around, there's no sign of
life

Voices, another sound, can you hear me now?

This is planet earth, you're looking at planet
earth..."

"Sexy Identities 10: A Monster By Any Other Name"

written by Max D

Featuring the Lovers of Sexy Identities

"Sexy Identities 10: A Monster By Any Other Name"
themes: MF, Romance, Furry, Implied Vaginal Sex

This is not me. I'm wearing my human suit right now, and I never feel quite, well, like myself dressed to look like all these people around me. I feel constrained and trapped and ready to burst while desperately trying to hide away. Yeah, I know. I'm thirty-one, and I should be used to pretending to be just like any other woman in the crowd. Sometimes I do better at it than others, but he could tell with just one look. That's all it took to see past my careful facade and the deliberate obfuscation of my real identity.

I was sitting on my usual perch at the coffee shop

"Sexy Identities 10: A Monster By Any Other Name"

and trying desperately to look normal on the outside. When I'm anxious, I need certain things to soothe my nerves. Otherwise my tummy gets twisted in knots and I get physically ill. What could I do though? I'd been let go from my old job, and I was interviewing twice a day to try and get something before I ran out of cash to pay my bills. I don't have much, but my little bolthole away from the crazies is everything to me. I can't ever go back to my mother asking me to stop being strange every morning. I can't ever go back to my father's disappointed frown each time he notices that I exist. My world was teetering on the edge of collapse, everything I had done to establish my own space was threatened, and I was panicking hard without even the tiniest bit of fur muff to run my fingers over and soothe my anxiety.

At the same time, I was outwardly trying to project confidence and leadership and whatever else it took to convince the manager that I was the one that he needed to run his team. I hate interviews where they make you wait ages to actually talk through your resume and qualifications. I know that it's intentional and used to see whether a candidate is patient and can handle frustration well. I was fighting the urge to chew on my long black hair when an older man pulled back a chair and sat at my table.

I was immediately thinking, "No no no no!" The last thing I needed while waiting to be interviewed was some old dude hitting on me. I clicked my mary janes together, and tried to look out the window, but he was definitely studying me. When I tried to scoop up my notepad and pen and the manila folder with my resume, I expected him to grab my arm or something. I was freaking out because my nerves were already shot, and he had deliberately inserted himself into what I imagined was my personal bubble.

He set his coffee on the table. "Hey," he said softly and relaxed while settling into his chair. "I'm guessing more of a cat person." I froze and he sighed. "It's ok. I just didn't want to sit by myself. I've been traveling a lot, and I was grateful to see one of my people after weeks on the road."

I tried my best bitchy glare, and he just smirked while making a wiping motion across the hair of his goatee. Instantly self-conscious, I tried to wipe off whatever I might have spilled on myself. There was nothing there. He was a jerk. "I was enjoying sitting by myself." I smiled despite how I felt. If the manager was watching then I wanted to make a good impression. At the same time, I gunned him down with lasers shooting from my hazel eyes. "I..."

He cut me off with a nod of his head directed toward where the coffee shop manager now seemed very distracted and was glancing in our direction while holding a stack of cups in his hand. "You need a reference? Tell me your three best skills and one thing that you've always wanted to be." His eyes never left mine, and there were stars twinkling within his glasses that I hoped were just a trick of the light passing through the windows. "Three best first. With confidence. You know yourself better than anyone else after all."

"Sexy Identities 10: A Monster By Any Other Name"

I didn't realize that he had tipped forward and placed his forearms on the table we shared until he slipped back into the comfort his chair's embrace and sipped his coffee. "I'm very smart," I said quietly. And, having said it without a thought, I was totally paralyzed because I couldn't figure out how to follow up on such a boastful statement.

"Of course, you are," he smiled. "You anticipate what needs to be done. You understand how to think things out. You've always been a little uneasy around strangers, so you think through what to do and how to do it until you're certain that you've got a good plan to follow." He was nodding, the manager was staring, and I was trapped. "Then reality happens. Just like this. You prefer to settle things peacefully. You don't enjoy confrontation. You'll do what you must to get things done. Sometimes, maybe, you should stand up for yourself more. You just want everyone taken care of, and you can sort out the rest for yourself." He seemed to see right through me, and, with a nod, ran a hand over his head with enough force to tug on his short clippered hair and scalp.

It was that gesture that opened my eyes. I stared at him, fiddled with the ends of my long hair, looked at the table in front of us, and then stared at him some more. He was easily half again my age with white shot through his goatee and mustache. His receding hairline had long since merged with a bald spot on the crown of his head. The straggling survivors of his long years spent amongst humans clung to the top of his bare scalp like lone sentries struggling to maintain their post. The hair that curled around his temples was white and grey and brown, and there were uneven sections where the hair seemed to flow against the natural direction that it should. He had, admittedly, a wild crazy eyebrow hair or two as well.

"I'm Lela," I said softly and held out my hand. He gave my fingers a brief squeeze and nodded. "What do you mean 'one of your people?'"

"Max," he replied. With quick eyes, he surveyed the room and double-checked on the manager who was now fumbling with napkins and stirring straws to justify coming close enough to listen to our conversation. "I know when I asked you to meet me, you said that you needed to be here for an interview. I hope I'm not too late. Your resume?" He pulled my manila folder to him, and I was utterly lost as he took control of everything without ever doubting that I would play along. "See, here," he pointed to my objectives, "I was intrigued by how you emphasized working to make things better for others. I don't read that sort of thing often, and I look at hundreds of resumes every year."

"Ummm, well, I think that it's important." He was giving me a chance to shine and setting up a competition between himself and the manager eavesdropping on us. I could see it in how he moved with deliberate pauses as he skimmed my resume with his pointing finger. "When people know they will be supported and taken care of then they work their best."

"Sexy Identities 10: A Monster By Any Other Name"

"Aren't you worried about spoiling them? People are naturally lazy if they can get away with it. How would you keep them in line when they know you won't confront them head on?"

It was a hard question, and the challenge sucked me in. "Good people aren't lazy. They want to know their work matters. They want to take pride in what they've done." In hindsight, he had baited me and drawn me out, and I was no longer thinking about my rent payment or his sudden appearance. "A good manager schedules people and cross-trains them so everyone works together as a team. You can't always hire good people, but you can mentor even the weakest team members so they can contribute. You have to focus on the best of each person."

He nodded slowly, digesting my words, and then asked, "And what brings out the best in you? My projects can be stressful with a lot of new territory to cover. I do things that no one has thought to do yet. I need maturity and insight from someone working closely with me because I don't always remember to care about feelings." He pushed my resume back to me and stretched out in his seat. "I may be a bit bold as well. I'm not fearless, but I understand that paranoia is a means to heighten my awareness and not a weakness that gets in my way."

"You asked a question," I replied while pushing my hair back. It was my turn to take charge, lean forward into the dark brown tabletop, and drive home my points. "Let me answer it." He nodded and waited patiently. "I do my best when I can be myself. I'm always willing to learn and I appreciate coaching and mentoring, but at the end of the day, I see the world from my perspective. That is probably different from yours and other people's views - which is why I'm a valuable addition to every team that I've worked on. I see what no one expects, and if you listen to my input then you benefit from that. I do not appreciate being treated as less of a person because I am a hardworker and do my best for people who need me and respect me. I know there are things you might be doing that I don't have much experience with, but I'm a very fast learner and I enjoy reading and studying new things."

I stopped myself to give him a chance to ask me a question, but he only had one and it put a big grin on my face. "Are you really going to let all your talents get sucked dry in a place like this? I'd hire you in an instant if you could commit to a two month trial period."

Before I could answer, the coffee shop manager interrupted us. "Ummm," he said uneasily and we both looked up at him in his green apron and white shirt, "I'm sorry that I was busy, Lela. Do you have time to talk now?" He looked very nervous despite the mod hairstyle and skinny jeans that marked him as a fashionable metrosexual in the suburbs type.

The older man across the table from me smirked, pulled out his wallet, and pushed a business card over to me after writing something on it. "It was my pleasure, Lela. I'm staying at a hotel all week. Please call and we'll do dinner. Or go for a long walk. I'd like to hear your back story and understand what makes you happy." Nodding at the manager, Max stood up and there was a glaring contrast between his restrained intensity and the younger man's superficial control. "I apologize for eating into your time. I hope you have a great discussion with Lela. I've been scouting her for a few months, and if you hire her then she will make a big change for the positive here. I'm certain of it."

It was not what he said about me, but how he said it. The words didn't matter. The manager and I both reacted to the soothing tones, the inherent faith, and it was impossible to not believe in his confident assessment. Even for me - and I knew that he was a complete stranger who had glanced over my resume in less than three minutes and asked me only a few questions. What I didn't know then was how good a read Max has about most people, especially people like me, because his paranoia attunes him to every possible threat or potential risk in a room.

My discussion with the coffee shop manager was very brief and uninspiring. Half of it came off as memorized sales pitches on why franchise coffee shops are so successful. The other half was somewhere between begging me to sign up and hard selling me on a start date. I was painfully aware that I needed the income. I was also fidgeting with the business card in my hand, and that was making it really hard to commit.

Before I just outright said I wasn't interested, I looked at the card more closely. When Max had passed it over, he had scribbled something beside his number. I had presumed it was the hotel he was staying at, but a quick glance made me laugh. The manager was expecting to be rejected - he had those sad puppy dog eyes going - and I gave the impression of giving in to his begging. We set my start date for the following day so I could get trained and collect a paycheck by the end of the week. Within minutes, I was buried under forms and paperwork, and I was still grinning when I turned them in half an hour later and said I'd be back in the morning.

Max was waiting for me on a bench facing the parking lot. It was impossible to mistake him because the glare of the sun off his exposed scalp was blinding. He must have watched my shadow approaching because he patted the bench seat and slid over to make room for me. "So was I right? More of a cat person? It can be hard to figure out what someone really looks like when they're all covered up." I perched on the bench and he looked me over while shielding the sun from his eyes.

In an earlier time, Max tells me, I would have grown up with fur coats and leather gloves. At most, I would have been considered to have a fur fetish in decades after that. I might not even have developed my unique self-identity. "A koala," I said softly. "Not a cat person." He just smiled, and I smiled back. "Was it really that obvious?" Maybe I wasn't so good at pretending to be human after all.

"Attractive woman. Experienced and mature. Under stress and anxious. She's struggling to not do something. She's trying to not be different. It's something I notice very quickly. Most people are oblivious to us even existing."

It was my turn and I hate guessing games. "Just tell me." He winked mischievously, and I shook a finger at him. "It better not be raven spelled R-H-A-V-Y-N or something silly like that." It was easy to make fun, but I could tell he was deadly serious, and it was a little scary.

"I'm a monster," he nodded his head as the words curled around my chest. "We don't presume to be any one thing. Monsters can be whatever they need to be." I was unconsciously inching away from him. There was no denying the gravity of his words, and I believed him unconditionally. There was something unnatural about his everything, and it was plain to see once I stopped pretending there was an older man sitting beside me. "Except human. We suck at that, too, apparently," and his deep rumbling chuckle was hardly any comfort.

"Hmmmm... ok." I wanted a fast exit, but Max was studying me closely, and I couldn't tell if it was safe to run away. Sometimes fleeing just inspires a predator to chase its prey. "Thanks for the recommendation, I guess."

He closed his eyes, sighed, and his face was scrunched up with concern and dismay. "Sorry. You asked. You were honest with me, so I didn't want to lie in response to a direct question. I'm sorry someone hurt you." His eyes looked down, and I tried to hide my wrists by pulling my long sleeves to my palms. "I liked your answers back in the coffee shop. You try to do the right thing for people, and that's really rare."

"Maybe you could try the same." I felt vulnerable and exposed, and it never occurred to me at the time that smarting off at a self-proclaimed monster was both self-defeating and pretty insane. He just shrugged it off and I got up to go. "You can have this back." I offered him his card.

Max didn't take it from my fingers though. "It was deadwood the moment I passed it to you. I just wanted to encourage you to accept the position and keep looking for better work. If you wanted to work with me then you would have stood up for yourself and let that manager know that he'd missed his opportunity." He got to his feet as well, and I suddenly realized that he was shorter than I am. "Hang onto it. Add me on LinkedIn or keep in touch somehow. I've never met a koala before. Pretty cool." With a gentle squeeze of his fingers to close my hand around his card, he walked away.

If I hadn't been so obviously disturbed then Max would have asked for a photo with me. That's one of his things. He doesn't want to forget the good stuff, especially since his brain is wired to always focus on risks and hazards. I called him that evening to apologize, feeling bad for being so abrupt with a stranger who had obviously tried his best to calm me down and help me get a job that I really needed. He answered and we start talking. He seemed distant though, and I knew that I had hurt his feelings. It all kind of came out then.

"Sexy Identities 10: A Monster By Any Other Name"

If you're like me then you know the conversation that I had with Max. You know my side of the story because it's your story, too. About always being different. About always being strange. About always being treated poorly and harassed and bullied. About not feeling safe. About knowing honesty gets you made fun of or worse. About trying to hide from so many things. About, well, not being human and being so uncomfortable pretending to be something that you aren't.

He understood all of it. He listened while I poured out my life story, and he asked questions here and there which made it clear that he cared. About me. About a total stranger. Because I was one of his people. Except, he really is a monster. He comes from the forests, from where civilization doesn't exist, and his ability to pull off such a successful act of subterfuge while openly stating that he's not a primate and not human is proof of how deeply he believes in himself. I'd like to say that I've never seen what he really means, but I have. I can't ever forget it, but I can also never forget what happened afterward. It's knowing that he cares that matters so much more, and people who care sometimes must do terrible things.

At the moment when I truly saw what a monster is capable of, I was shaking in terror. I was rooted to the floor and couldn't leave. I was afraid for my life. And he stopped, in slow motion, and wrapped an arm around me. With a growl that made my neck hairs stand on end, he savagely pummeled someone dumb enough to charge at him. In a voice so soft that it could have been the wind whispering through leaves, he asked me if I wanted to go while his powerful heart hammered in his chest and his flexing muscles dared the primates to attack him again while one of their own was sprawled out on the floor sobbing and clutching at his shattered torso.

He guided me to the door, leaving behind ruin and chaos, and the bouncers confronted him right as we were almost out of the club. They were roaring and hollering, trying to bring him down with the force of their thundering rage, and he simply eased me ahead of him and whispered that he'd need a minute. I didn't let the door shut because I was terrified that I would never see him again. I watched as half a dozen men joined the bouncers and were pointing and shouting and trying to grab at Max.

"We had a misunderstanding," he said with infuriating clarity and calm. "Your children thought I would tolerate being molested. Specifically those two," he pointed at two men pushing at the bouncers to get at him, "thought humiliating me in front of my cousin would somehow prove their machismo and win her affection. Their patsy is still in there. He won't heal quickly."

The faces of the bouncers were still contorted with fury, and they were flexing their arms while pushing back on the gang seeking to get at Max. They heard him loud and clear. They heard an older white man being condescending to them and the regulars that they had known for years. One of them was jawing at Max, the words were full of commands and invectives, but the monster didn't even seem to notice. He was something else, something separate, and that incited even more intense hatred from the shouting mob.

"So I suggest," his plain spoken words had no accent or regional tone, "that you help them understand that if they insist on asserting their existence anywhere near me again then I will gladly hospitalize them so they can learn humility and compassion through years of personal suffering." It was something in his voice and expression. The way he didn't need to look away from the massive bouncers or the pushing and hollering crowd. He was from nowhere. He was not one of their kind. They had made a mistake, but only he saw it that way.

One of the men spit in his face. I saw it happening. The bouncers were too slow. They couldn't honestly prevent something from happening. The men crowded behind their big bodies could have gotten to Max easily if they tried. I guess Max had known that all along. He expected the passive-aggressive assault, a deliberate act of defiance meant to demean him, and, as I said, he can read people so very well because he always expects the worst.

With the precision of a knife, Max jabbed into the man's face with stiff fingers that evoked howling and screeching. "An eye for an eye," he growled before stepping backward through the open door. I didn't want to look down to see what he was shaking off his fingers. He was closely watching the bouncers' bodies, if I had to guess based on his tucked chin and the swivel of his head, and he clearly wanted to shift the confrontation to a more open setting. "If you want more, children, then come outside where there is no one to hold you back."

The jeering mob didn't follow us out. One of the bouncers did, but as soon as he made like he was going to push Max forward into the sidewalk, the sudden shift in Max's stance and his agile pivot to face the man twice his size established an unhappy detente. It didn't stop the big man from making his point though. "Get the fuck out. And don't come back. That would be a mistake." The bigger man squared off and stood like a waiting gladiator in front of the club's double doors.

Max shrugged and laughed. "Be sure to let James know that I had a good time." He name-dropped the club night's manager without a care in the world, and then he very casually removed his glasses and wiped off the spittle on his left lens. The bouncer went back into the club, pulling the double doors shut behind him, and the sidewalk was empty except for a few lost souls wandering from intersection to intersection with alcohol fueled intentions.

After he was put his glasses back on, his fingers carefully caressed my back. I sensed it was more than that. He was testing whether I rejected him because of his violent nature, and, when I didn't jump away from his touch, Max put an arm around me and we walked together toward where he was parked. "I'm sorry." Such simple words to convey so much meaning.

"Sexy Identities 10: A Monster By Any Other Name"

"You're a monster," it kept playing back in my head so saying it out loud helped.

"Truth.   What do koalas eat for comfort food? I'm feeling pretty battered and down."

I've seen what a monster can do, the violence and fury we anticipate, and my heart broke when I discovered what the price for being capable of so much is.   That is why Max is still a friend of mine.   I actually came to a full stop that night, planted my feet, and had to stare at him in the glaring light from the streetlamps while our reflections were dark shadows on the office fronts along the city avenue.   "What? You feel down?"   Even as I said the words, I could see it in his eyes.   He was hurt and upset.   He was uncomfortable in his own skin.   He was damaged beyond repair, punished for simply wanting to be on his own, and he had to wonder if even I would abandon him for not accepting abuse and harassment from others.

And I got it.   I finally understood.   It's not just that Max is a monster.   It's that being a monster is something that he is extraordinarily good at.   He has all these tricks and shortcuts and ways to do things that no one has ever even thought of.   He takes charge and doesn't let anyone stop him when he knows that he's right.   He suffers the burden of knowing that he'll be the last man standing because others don't have the fortitude and endurance to keep him company on the journey that he has undertaken all these long years.   We reject him while trying to claim our own right to exist.   We are frightened by him because he's different. He's a monster because that's what he is, yet he lives in a world where the rules are in place for sheep because they might get a bit rowdy and hurt themselves. The herd can't tell him from a barbed wire fence, and they're too self-enamoured to realize both are very real dangers but he is not a passive obstacle in the path of their bleating stampede. Amongst our own kind, we can't tell him apart from other predators, and so we spurn him even when he's trying to protect us.

"I'm so sorry," I whispered. And I'm not a monster. I'm not tough like him. I wrapped my arms around his body, his heat soaking into my black tank top, and I cried while holding him tight. Max doesn't need to have scars on his wrists to prove his suffering. His heart is where he has harmed himself over and over again just to survive. Isolation is the blade he uses to cut into flesh and bone, severing sinew and tendon, and his scars are so apparent that no one sees them at all. "I was so scared."

I remember him slowly walking me backward but never pushing me away. I remember him murmuring to me about how everyone needs someone. I remember knowing that he meant I needed someone but he would never have that. I remember him opening my door and easing me into the passenger seat. I remember him being so quiet when he usually talks forever after going out dancing. I remember dozing off in his rental car with my head on his shoulder and hand on his leg.

When he half carried me from the parking garage to the hotel lobby, I depended on his strength to hold me up. When he held me close, I kissed him to thank him for caring. As he guided me to his bed, I beckoned him to join me with open arms. I ignored the worry in his heart, the expectation of rejection, and I wrapped myself around him. His strong arms lifted me up as I wiggled out of my skirt. I nearly headbutted him as I pulled off my black tank top and fishnet shirt. I laughed as he tickled my feet after helping me out of my New Rock boots. He was still dressed in his tactical trousers and snug fitting Under Amour shirt when I was down to my bra and panties and cuddling him as best a koala can.

He reached for something and I fought the urge to tug him back to me. I thought he was checking his phone, but instead he pulled a fur muff from a shopping bag beside the bed. I was in heaven as he petted me, the softness caressing every curve of my body, and I held it tight in my hands as he undressed. He's older than me, but I never notice once the lights go out. It's the experience of his touch and how easily he finds all the sensitive places that rarely get attention that sucks me in. When his fingers gently capture and pinch my nipples, I'm already breathing hard and scratching his back. I'm so ready as his kisses flow over my neck and his goatee and mustache rough up my soft skin. He slips between my thighs, teasing me, and I want so much more.

I've seen what a monster can do. Between my legs as I gasped and shook beneath him, his powerful arms holding him up so his body only made contact with mine when I arched my back and thrust myself onto him. His physical stamina pushed me past my limits, and I went further and further without knowing when my pleasure would end. He left me exhausted and sore, softly teased me for hugging his fur gift to my bare breasts, and then wrapped his arms around me. Facing each other while lying on our sides, his body warmed mine. Spooning into my back later, his desire throbbed against my pale buttocks. Any other man, I'd have worried about what might happen in my sleep. With Max, I wondered how quickly I could recharge so he could enjoy my eagerness even more.

That night was years ago, but it seems like yesterday. The venom and fury of his aggression followed by the stillness of his breath in a quiet hotel room overlooking the city never left me. I lost touch, stopped responding to his messages, and then he came to me with this idea out of nowhere. He was going to write about us. He was going to talk about what we need and what we love and what we feel. And I knew right from the start that Max was really writing about me and my sisters and brothers. He was trying to help explain something that he sees so clearly and has always appreciated. So I wanted to write about him. So you would understand.

These stories are about those of us who put on our human suits, who try to fit in, and who were lucky enough to meet a man who is a monster. We each have our fetishes. We each have our desires. We each have our accessories and costumes and insane passions. In a way, he has all of that and none of it. His fetish is for the improbable and deliciously deviant and amazingly unlikely. We're the ones that he always notices. We're the ghosts that haunt him. We're the one hope that he thinks might save the species. We're the ones that he feels are worth fighting for.

He's not just dealing with the mobs of primates though. He doesn't expect to be saved when the time comes. I hate to think of what sort of demons and angels that a monster believes in, but I have learned certain things in Max's company. Beware the heart of a monster that has lived long enough amongst men to be welcomed into their homes and offices without a second thought. Even for those of us that are different, our anger is just a storm. His anger is a raging hurricane. For us, our love is a comfort. Love to him is blessed mana. For us, our pain is frailty and doubt. His pain is shattered bones and yet he perseveres with purpose alone to straighten his limbs and forever remember the suffering of each misstep and each blow. The passions of monsters may require the scourges and violence of the Old Testament to be brought to heel because I can't imagine anything else bringing him down.

Those Old Testament days are in the past though.

And there are no gods nor goddesses to stop monsters now.

Cherish Desire Creators

Our Creators

Cherish Desire works with amazing skilled and experienced writers, editors, narrators, video narrators, models, photographers, musicians, and muses to create written, audio, and video content along with the supporting graphics, trailers, and music clips. While Max tackles the majority of assembling their contributions into a finished format, Cherish Desire would be a lot less without their involvement.

Max

Max is the go to guy for those crazy sex questions that only come up during a night of drinking - because he "just knows that stuff" and he doesn't drink. When not receiving text messages with queries about British boys wearing unicorn suits and SMS messages with wine bottle adventure photos, Max wanders North America and Western Europe music festivals and clubs so he can dance his own way. His sexy companions try to keep him in line, and his work tries to keep him too busy to get into trouble - but Max is an unrestrainable phenomena orthogonal to the Zeitgeist.

That's the official blurb anyway. Here's a little bit more since you've read this far.

I remember walking along the river in HafenCity in Hamburg, das Fuchs and I taking photos at different angles to highlight the Elbphilharmonie, while laughing about "Pride and Prejudice and Zombies," and the wind swept over us with whispers of impending rain. I spent an afternoon with the Mistress of Wiesbaden at Kloster Eberbach, wandering the abbey after walking the grounds, before driving along the Rhein to take her home. The loud conversations in a pizzeria, the soft accent of Wien drifting into the night, and the pause as a cluster of departing friends share one last set of shots. A week later, looking down over Los Angeles from the Griffith Observatory as black helicopters circle overhead, Mistress Militia enthusing about her drag queen shows and posing for photos. That night laughing with the Chicago crew at Das Bunker while our friends, Alter Der Ruine, play a final show, and the Portland crew is meowing and dancing in the middle of the crowd for the headline band. There's no time for sleep until I get back to Orlando, and then it's time for work a couple of hours after the red eye lands. Life continues without a pause button everywhere - and the music slows before building up to another crescendo.

The past is a collision of what we knew and where we've been. Perspective rewrites the narrative, and we discover new truths amongst old experiences. Over time, the drift of passions leads people to different ends. Perhaps we can finally accept that people are not meant to be interchangeable parts and they don't have to be cut and shaped to fit into specific shapes and forms. Probably not. I don't think the center of the bell curve is ready to admit the rest of us exist. No offense. We've never been their kind.

So there are these stories. The Mistress of Wiesbaden likes to say that each one is a chance to sit back, close her eyes, and wander through the imagination of friends. Of course, she's a big fan of imagination as long as she gets to satisfy her natural passions for destruction and domination. Some of them are only a moment expressed in a furious detonation of confrontation and resolution. Many more are the edges and outlines of a bigger world.

By way of introduction, none of these are the reality of Max or Ronin or Tom. You meet them and their companions bit by bit. You get a chance to watch their affairs and their fights. They can't possibly tell you everything, so instead you have to learn about them through what happens. Sometimes, they know more than you'd expect. Other times, they're as lost as the rest of us. Pieces fall into place, and they are just as likely to jump to conclusions as the silent stalkers reading about them. There's no easy way in or out of the desires and chaos of life. Time passes but some things stay the same. It's never clear whether this is how they escape their limits or how they define their choices, but it doesn't take much to figure out that they're doing the best they can.

Stepping back, Cherish Desire as a whole -

whether we're talking about Very Dirty Stories, Very Wicked Dirty Stories, Singles, or Divinations - is a project that's about alternate voices. If EL James can play make believe and write poorly about a scene which she clearly doesn't belong in then why can't we write about the actual fetish parties we attend? If the media desperately wants to portray a world full of fear and danger at every turn with only religious belief to save them then maybe it's time for the masses to discover what we believe in - and that's a much broader pantheon of gods and demons and shapeshifters and elementals than they are probably prepared for. If we must live within the surveillance states demanded by our fellow citizens then why not accept the perversion of our bondage and submission to the devices we hold in our hands?

While some people want comfort, want direction, and want closure, I'm guessing there's a bigger audience for people who want the rush and to unleash the primal energies they suppress every day and night. That can get brutal. Emotions happen. People do get hurt. They fall in love. Companions stumble into anger and frustration. Friends fight back. Some decisions change everything.

Maybe yours did as well.

Cherish Desire Erotica

Very Dirty Stories

We wanted to share our favorite sex stories. The ones that broke out of the conventional erotica mold, shattered the limitations of casual romance and sex, and dove into detailed and realistic action involving stretching, large sex toy play, vaginal and anal fisting, domination, fantasy monster and animal dildo play, restraints and suspension, elaborate medical and DIY devices, and more. We did it bit by bit, discovering and learning as we went, and released volume after volume of two to five short stories to challenge readers to be sexually aroused by something truly intense or charmingly subtle. Very Dirty Stories volumes are about ladies that expose themselves and embrace their fears and desires as well as the men and women that inspire them to sexual peaks while living out wild sexual fantasies.

Singles

We wanted to publish sexual adventures that were more than a one night stand. So we gathered together our favorite ladies and delightfully sexy themes and created Singles - longer collections of sexual stories that fit together to cover formative physical and psychological experiences that define her womanhood or establish a collection of deviant delights and sexual alternatives. These trailblazing erotica books go deeper, harder, faster, and expose the soft white underbelly of sensual need while delivering thrust after thrust of sexual intensity and the soothing pleasures of passionate affection. Explore the explicit erogenous zones of women and their sexual partners. Be prepared for sexually challenging situations as well as character details that get beyond height, weight, hair colour, and favorite size of dildo. Plunge into their stories and get wet. Singles also make great gifts for that secret someone who needs a sexual swift kick in the nuts or a perverse surprise stashed for long trips and evenings in.

~~Very~~ Wicked Dirty Stories

The darkness of desires are shadows always encircling the hope of fulfillment and pleasure. These are the twisted realities fueled by the uninhibited passions and believes of the few. Their sexual urges, their powerful alliances, and their willingness to defend their own as well as to strike out and forcefully embrace what they require. ~~Very~~ Wicked Dirty Stories hint at the unobserved and strange frayed edges of reality that we like to censor or ignore. Ghosts, shapeshifters, and great powers linger just beyond the firelight while watching humanity sleep.

Divinations

Cherish Desire Divinations erotica delves into darkness. Lusty shapeshifters, impassioned spirits, dangerous players, and perverse pagan deities beckon with sordid promises and unseemly urges. Their intense passions expose their bestial and heavenly natures while emphasizing how closely they represent unfettered hunger, cunning, love, and wickedness. Divinations was born of fevered imaginations and sexual abandonment that left us aching, bruised, and hoping for more. Divination books are collections of erotic stories that go deep and explore psycho-sexuality as well as physical modifications suited to the nearly immortal. The limited disguise of humanity has been stripped away, and the results are animalistic sexual rituals and self-enlightened spirituality that arouse jaded desires for more.

Cherish Desire apologizes in advance for exposing the true nature of shapeshifters and the transcendent hungers that lurk behind every door and under every bed.

Discover More

For our complete catalog of titles, explore our books: https://wulf.fun/CherishDesireErotica

For more about your favorite characters, check out the ladies: https://wulf.fun/CherishDesireLadies

Very Dirty Stories, ~~Very~~ Wicked Dirty Stories, Cherish Desire Singles, and Cherish Desire Divinations titles include over 450 erotica stories to delight even the most jaded readers. With a focus on perverse desires that push limits to achieve blissful pleasure, intense action and taboo desires inspire fantasies and arousal for a satisfying climax.

The majority of Cherish Desire titles are available in digital editions with audio, video narration, and paperback editions for select stories and books.

And when you visit the Cherish Desire Catalog, get elite and a free eBook from Cherish Desire by signing up for the inside track.

Printed in Great Britain
by Amazon